THE
PRODIGAL

THE PRODIGAL

Philip Hughes

World Wide

A ministry of the Billy Graham Association

1303 Hennepin Avenue
Minneapolis, Minnesota 55403

The Prodigal

The Prodigal, © 1983, World Wide Publications.
Published by World Wide Publications, 1303 Hennepin
Avenue, Minneapolis, Minnesota 55403.

Printed in U.S.A.

Library of Congress Cataloging in Publication Data:

Hughes, Philip
   The Prodigal

   1. Fiction   I. Title

83-050462

ISBN 0-89066-048-4

And the son said to him, "Father, I have sinned against heaven and before you; I am no longer worthy to be called your son."

But the father said to his servants, "Bring quickly the best robe, and put it on him; and put a ring on his hand, and shoes on his feet; and bring the fatted calf and kill it, and let us eat and make merry; for this my son was dead, and is alive again; he was lost, and is found."

And they began to make merry.

Luke 15:21-24 (RSV)

1

"Excuse me, have you seen anyone that looks like this?"
The man behind the bar reluctantly accepted the photograph and stepped into the beam of an overhead light. Stone-faced, he examined it and turned back to the owner.

"Who is he?"

"His name's Greg Stuart. I'm trying to find him."

"I gathered that."

"He hasn't been seen for a while."

The bartender took a long drag on a cigarette and tucked a swinging, gold medallion back inside his shirt. Music blared from enormous speakers.

"Who are you?"

"Pardon?"

He leaned close and raised his voice an octave. "Watch my lips carefully, please. I asked, 'Who are you?' "

"Scott Stuart. I'm   "

"His brother, right?"

Scott nodded and took the photo back.

"Sorry. I can't help you. Half of Boeing comes through here every day."

A dancer had emerged onto a stage to an outburst of hoots and whistles. Scott felt the floor throb to the deafening sounds. The thick smoke in the air hurt his eyes.

"Get you a beer? Anything?"

Shaking his head, Scott pocketed the photograph and started toward the door. The people packed into the dark bar seemed one faceless mass.

Scott climbed into his blue Toyota Land Cruiser and gunned off, leaving a trail of exhaust, threading his way through traffic. At the second red light, he realized he was just driving aimlessly and pulled into a parking lot. He killed the engine, leaned back in the seat, inhaled slowly, and blew out a long breath. A sense of frustration descended on him. The search for his 21-year-old brother had yielded nothing thus far, not even the feeling of "getting warm." Trying to be methodical, he took out his checklist and scratched off another possibility. Platitudes about needles in haystacks and wild goose chases floated into his mind. A new idea replaced them.

The bartender had mentioned Boeing. Why, he wondered, had he not called the huge corporation to see if Greg had gotten a job there? He had ignored the obvious. Scott drove along Beacon Avenue until he saw a fast food restaurant. Inside, a waitress, with a ketchup stain on her dress and earrings like hula hoops, changed a dollar for him. A puffy-faced salesman had just finished a call. Having found the main office number in the phone directory, Scott plunked himself down at the pay phone and slipped in a coin.

"Can you hold, please?" said a voice. He was instantly cut off before he could reply. After a series of clicks, another voice came on.

"I'm sorry, sir. We are not accepting applications at this time."

Scott explained that he was looking for Greg Stuart, his brother.

"And is Mr. Stuart employed by Boeing Aircraft?"

"That is what I am trying to find out."

"I'm sorry, sir. I don't have that information."

They rerouted him to personnel, who told him flatly that Boeing employed no one named Greg Stuart.

Disappointed but undaunted, Scott looked again at his list. There were four telephone numbers of Greg's friends. It was late enough that they might be home from work or school. The salesman was returning to the phone. Pretending he had not seen him, Scott quickly inserted a coin and began tapping buttons.

According to a recorder, the first number was "no longer in service," mechanically adding, "and there is no new number." Ignoring the presence of the salesman, Scott crossed off that number and dialed the next. A voice came from behind.

"Excuse me, are you going to be using this phone for long? I have an important call to make."

With his finger, Scott hung up in mid-number, dug out his dime, and turned around.

"I'm trying to locate my brother. I have a list of people to call. Probably be here a while."

The salesman frowned, shrugged, then departed. Scott tried the next number. A former friend of Greg's had not seen him for some time. He urged Scott to notify him when he found Greg because, "He owes me money."

Scott crossed out another lead and called again. One of Greg's ex-girl-friends blabbed at him for several minutes. She said she had not seen him since a party some weeks ago, then volunteered a list of suggestions for the search, all of which Scott had already tried. "Maybe he works for Boeing?" she said. One more call, Scott told himself, remembering his heavy load of studies. The tones of the numbers played a little tune through the receiver.

"Greg?" answered a monotone male voice. "How is he doing anyway?" Scott explained that Greg had been missing for several months.

"A friend of mine said he thought he saw him in a store."

"Where?" Scott milked him for all possible details, scrawling them down on a steno notebook; last off-ramp on Interstate 5 before Everett, small market, Don's, or something similar.

"You know, a guy like Greg could be anyplace, really," the friend said. "It's a big world out there." Scott agreed and hung up, thankful for a clue—any clue—however vague, to go on.

SPEED CHECKED BY RADAR

Noting the sign, Scott slowed down the engine from a whine to an even hum. The car needed a muffler. Heading north on the Interstate, he stared around constantly, in hopes of a miraculous glimpse of his brother. Someone in a crowded car flashed half a peace sign at him for his trouble. A faded bumper sticker ahead of him proclaimed: I FOUND IT! The heavy traffic thinned slightly past Ballinger Road. Scott watched for the exit. His engine spit as he coasted down the ramp. The sign loomed on the left.

DON'S MINI-MART AND DELI
SPECIALS
ON BUDS & CIGS

This would be the last stop for the day.

"No, haven't seen him," a teenage girl said, hanging on to the picture. "Your brother? He's cute. I'd remember someone like that. I'm only part-time. Why don't you ask Don?" She pointed with her nose.

A balding man lounged behind a counter, reading a glossy magazine. His look reminded Scott of people's expressions when he came collecting for the paper route he had as a child.

"He looks like a thousnd people who come in here. Does look a little familiar, though," he said on further scrutiny.

"Wish I could tell you for certain."

Scott explained his search, that Greg had been seen in this store, and that the parents were worried.

"Oh, I can understand your situation," Don said. "I've got the same trouble myself."

A wry smile swept across the proprietor's mouth. Scott, with an inquiring expression, leaned toward the man for an explanation. Don picked up the magazine from which Scott's inquiries had detoured him, and opened to a centerfold of a voluptuous model, clad only in a diaphanous scarf.

"Could you possibly tell me where *she* lives?" he asked with a laugh.

Scott left the store with a sense of futility. He heard the laugh boom again from inside, as he got into the car. The sun had begun to set. He stopped a moment before driving off. The bulk of the city lay to the south. To the west and north spread miles of bays, forests, and mist-shrouded islands where entire regiments, if they so desired, could remain hidden for years. Scott wondered if the one sighting of Greg—and a dubious one at that—justified searching the remote regions.

On the way home, he let an all-news station clutter his mind. Near his ramshackle walk-up apartment in the industrial section, billows of smoke funneled up from a stack into an acrid, rotten-smelling cloud. The paper mill fumes always made him cough. Hungry and remembering his empty refrigerator, he stopped and bought a hamburger. He was late; a rusty, dented Olds had usurped his usual parking place. The fifth step on the first set of stairs gave its customary creak. From other apartments, he heard strains of television shows, clanking dishes and too-shrill voices. Entering his own flat, he called his parents, eating as he talked. A mountain of school assignments sat on the desk. Scott told all that had transpired, knowing that his mother would immediately deduce the results. The inflection of worry and hurt in her voice brought to his mind a vision of her face. If the distinct possibility that Greg had been seen lifted her spirits at all, he could not tell. A long break of silence followed. Scott cleared his throat.

"I'm going to poke around up on the Sound next week, after my Greek exam."

Again visualizing the face at the other end, he infused his voice with confidence he did not really feel.

"I'll find him."

2

Anne replaced the receiver. The click echoed through the house, as if the dwelling were an empty concert hall. The place had always seemed excessively large; it now struck her as cavernous. Sitting alone, she tried to define her feelings. Earlier that day, while cleaning, she had felt like an employee. The conversation with Scott lingering in her mind, she could not avoid the sense of feeling bilked of something, deprived of a birthright by whims of will and fate against which she stood powerless. She glanced outside. The street lay deserted, the house across the street dark. Silence grew audible. Anne turned on the radio to a classical station, rejected the strident music that emerged, and opted for a Joaquin Rodrigo album of her own selection. After several minutes, she vetoed this, too, and forced herself to read John Fowles' *Daniel Martin*, while she waited for Elton to come home. She heard the car door slam.

Elton's tall frame filled the open doorway. He moved slowly, deliberately, almost in sections. He carried himself as one conscious of his importance (and of being frequently in view of others), like a politician facing a television crew. His expression betrayed serious thought, as though he were about to issue a directive of great importance, or answer a complicated question. He embraced Anne, kissing her on the top of the head.

"May I just pause to catch my breath before we go?" he asked, unfolding himself on the green, flower-print sofa.

Anne, though hungry and fantasizing a favorite dish, sat in a chair opposite him.

"Of course. Do you want to see the mail?"

"Don't bother," replied Elton, stretching, joining his hands behind his head and shutting his eyes. "Unless, of course, there is something important?"

Anne knew what he meant. "No, just bills."

"You can spare me that. I can't even open bills anymore without getting heart failure. Makes me wonder how most people survive."

Elton paused as an idea occurred to him.

"You know, I've never thought of comparing some of last year's ..."

"Elton," Anne interrupted, "Scott called a little while ago."

He met her gaze, then looked off before speaking.

"What happened? Some felon break into that hovel of his?"

Elton put particular emphasis into the word *hovel.*

"No, he's been looking around for Greg."

"Well, did he find him? Did he see him?"

"No, he didn't see him—but someone else did."

"Where? Not in some ..."

"... in a store near Everett, just off the highway. Scott wants to look out on the Sound next week."

Elton looked blank, then started to say something. Anne cut him off.

"Do you know what he said to me, Elton? He told me, 'I'll find him.' And he sounded so sure about it."

Elton shook his head slightly and took a breath before speaking.

"Let's face it, Anne," he said, forehead furrowing, adding a rare, palms-up hand gesture. "He's not a child. If anyone like Greg does not want to be found, then that is quite simply the end of it. Scott's newfound 'faith' and free-lance sleuth work notwithstanding."

Elton rose from his chair, as if to say by this act, *discussion ended.*

"I don't know about you, but I'm ready to eat."

They left. A gentle rain had started, the drops sparkling as they entered the cones of light cast by the high street lamp. They said little to each other on the way to the restaurant. Elton hit his umbrella on the top of the doorway as they entered, and placed it in a receptacle provided for that purpose.

"Reservations for Stuart, please."

An elderly waiter ushered them to a corner table. As they sat down, the candle burning in the middle of the table flickered slightly, steadying into a perfect drop of flame. They scrutinized the menu, then ordered what they had eaten last time.

"I'm seriously considering some of that vacation property a few of my sales staff are so enthusiastic about. Up around Lake Wenatchee."

Anne half-listened.

"I've never been big on real estate, but it seems a solid enough investment. Prices keep going right up. Buyer's market, too, at this time of year, something else to consider."

"Wouldn't it be nice," replied Anne in a low voice, trying to follow the theme, "if we could all be skiing over Christmas?"

Anne's face reflected the candlelight. Elton caught himself staring at her, as if he had somehow forgotten her elegance and dignified beauty and momentarily rediscovered it. Her hair and face seemed to retain the light. The waiter brought beverages, breaking Elton's meditation.

"I think," Elton said, taking a short sip, "that the boys might have their own plans for over Christmas. One thing we do know." He set the glass down. "At least one of them does."

The statement seemed to linger in the air.

3

"**Y**our time is up."

The announcement, accompanied by several sharp raps on a desk, snapped Scott out of his train of thought. During the exam, time had seemed suspended. The professor, as expected, had loaded the test with obscure vocabulary and the trickiest verb tenses—pluperfect subjunctives and conditionals. In the translation section, Scott had pored over a difficult passage until the Greek letters looked like arrangements of bones that held some cryptic meaning. His eyes ached and his head felt as if it would explode. Most of the other students had finished earlier. He made sure his name was on the paper and handed it in. Doing so, he felt a great load tumble off his back. The professor, an austere-looking academic, flashed him a wink. Smiling, Scott left, hopeful that he had scored a decent grade.

A peal of bells from the chapel tower had the effect of cleaning his mind, starting him over, as he headed out to look for Greg. He tentatively planned to nose around the wharves at Salmon Bay before heading out to the Sound. His car's engine roared into life, turning several heads. It's exhaust leak had worsened during the week.

Out in the bay, ships called to each other, their *basso profundo* horns accompanying the sharp ambulance-cries of seagulls searching for food. The air smelled of fish and diesel fumes. Scott investigated a series of docked fishing boats. There did not seem to be much activity. He had brought the picture of Greg. It drew a blank from the first person he questioned, the captain of the trawler *Elusive*, a name, Scott considered, of some significance.

"Nope, sorry, can't help you."

The captain retreated onto his vessel, flicking a cigarette into the water, where it hissed out in a rainbow of oil film. Moving on, Scott stopped a fisherman who appeared elderly from a distance, but on closer inspection, proved a tired, unshaven youth of about twenty.

"Hi! Hey, I'm looking for my brother."

The youth smelled more like fish than a fish. He did not appear eager for conversation.

"I thought maybe he'd gotten some day work on one of the boats."

"Your brother, huh?" he said, returning the picture after a quick glance. "We'd use him for crab bait," he snapped.

"Right." The word seemed to pop out in lieu of a better comeback. Undiscouraged, Scott continued his seemingly fruitless search. *He must be in this area*, he thought.

Other inquiries brought similar results. Still undeterred, Scott drove a short way and tried one of the mills, though he thought Greg would be more likely to work on the water. A man operating an enormous front-end loader nearly bowled him over. He sat so high, Scott nearly had to yell. Scaling the machine, Scott showed the picture, but the operator replied with an emphatic negative almost before he had seen it.

"Thanks a lot, man." A growl of exhaust muted his words. *People don't care anymore*, he said to himself.

A group of workers on their coffee break regarded him at

first like an approaching policeman—then seemed to find him a novelty. They were all bearded; most wore lumberjack shirts, a few sported folding knives on their belts. Scott read one of their lettered T-shirts.

SKOAL—A PINCH IS ALL IT TAKES

They passed the photograph around, posing a series of questions of their own: "What are you, a cop? Is he a runaway? What's he wanted for? Rape? Ha! Ha! What happened? He forget to floss or something?" As Scott walked away, one of them lisped, "Do you mith your thweety?" A chorus of belly laughs followed.

Scott's instinct told him to keep trying the area. Other workers, although they had seen nothing, thought he was at least looking in the right place. He lost track of the number of people he questioned, and by the time he had finished, it was too late to fight the heavy Friday traffic heading out of town.

The next day, before sunup, Scott headed straight north on Interstate 5, bound for Mukilteo. He felt fresh, and bursting with energy, filled with renewed confidence. The city slept; the freeways were all but deserted. A transport truck with Montana plates passed him. Before turning off to Mukilteo, Scott tried Don's Deli on the chance that Greg might have stopped there again, but nobody had seen him. He bought a large coffee and a danish and took it with him.

AUTO FERRY TO WHIDBEY ISLAND ONE MILE

The ferry, with a light load of cars, made good time. When the ramp finally slammed down, Scott was ready to roll. He drove north on Highway 20, passing Coupeville and crossing the bridge at Deception Pass, where the waters of the Sound divided Whidbey from Fidalgo Island. He ruled out La Conner on the mainland for the present, thinking that it might be better to try it on the way back, if he had time. He kept on going to Anacortes and boarded the ferry for

Guemes. His first inquiry of another passenger brought a smart remark to the effect that he might as well be trying to capture Bigfoot. The rustic-looking man appeared to regret the quip and suggested Scott try the island store, where most islanders bought supplies.

The ferry slushed through the water. Scott stood, hands in his pockets, looking out at the scenery, but not seeing it. His mind had dredged up a scene from many years past.

He and Greg were children, seated in the front pew at church, surreptitiously elbowing and pinching each other. A youth choir sang about God, love, and happy days. Parents smiled and flashbulbs popped. The congregation, Elton and Anne prominent among them, showered the children with applause. Mrs. Frandsen, a Sunday School teacher, stood and announced a dramatization to be performed by the Junior Department. As she talked, Greg released a garter snake from his pocket. It writhed on the pew where the choir would sit, its tiny red tongue lashing in and out.

"Scott Stuart has written his own rendition of the timeless story of the prodigal son. His brother, Greg, will play the prodigal, and Billy Patterson will be the faithful father."

Insides trembling, Scott mounted the platform and read solemnly from lined tablet paper.

"This is a story from the Bible about a man who had two sons."

He stopped briefly and looked up, locating the beaming faces of his parents before continuing. Greg, dressed in a costume his mother probably thought was biblical, joined his brother at the front. Feeling more at ease, Scott read on with his best expression.

"The father was an upright citizen, and he had lots and lots of money in the bank. They were a happy family, until one day, the youngest son said to his father, 'I don't want to live here anymore! I want to do what *I* want to do! I want to see the world! Give me a lot of money!'"

Greg held out an open palm to Billy, who hesitated a moment before digging in his pockets and pressing a wad of money into Greg's hand.

"The father was sad," Scott read, "but he gave him the money anyway."

At this cue, Greg skipped along the aisle, past his parents, in whose faces he flashed his fortune in play money, and out the massive doors of the church.

"And he went far, far away to seek his fortune. Everybody at home missed him very much. He ..."

Screams broke the narrative. The choir, now seated in the pew, had discovered the snake. Scott saw Elton crane his neck to see what caused the commotion while his mother looked toward the doors, expecting to see Greg. He never appeared for his curtain call.

A belch from the ferry's whistle jerked Scott out of his nostalgia. He followed the lead of others and got into his car. The ramp slammed down. He drove directly to the island store.

The place seemed to belong to another century. Its grizzled proprietor, Mr. Marler, squinted at Greg's picture.

"I might'a seen 'im."

Scott felt a pang of hope.

"Lotsa folks through here in the summer. What you want him for?"

"I'm his brother." This drew a skeptical look. Mr. Marler compared faces. Scott quickly added, "Family needs him."

The old man's eyes combed Scott, evaluating.

"Please, I need your help." Scott held the old man's gaze.

"He cut a cord of wood for me a couple weeks back. Took his pay in canned goods."

A flurry of words swarmed to Scott's lips. He tried to stay calm.

"Did he say where he was going?"

The old man wrinkled up his face and spat copiously off to one side.

"Gotta feelin' he's out on Mahatka Island."

Scott suddenly felt a surge of euphoria.

"Thank you, Mr. Marler," he said, already in a sprint towards his car.

"You're an answer to prayer!"

"He's not supposed to be out there this time of year," the old man called after him.

Making a flying leap, Scott cut loose a whoop of joy that echoed off the trees. Barely under way, he realized his ignorance as to how to get to the island. He backed up and turned around, inquiring of Mr. Marler where he could rent a boat.

"Remember, he's not supposed to be out there this time a year," he repeated, as if the island were his precinct. The Land Cruiser's rear tires shot out stones as Scott left.

He balked at the small size of the rental boats, but the Sound lay as flat as he had ever seen it. Bearing straight for Mahatka, it occurred to him that he had not been reveling in the perfect weather. Everything seemed an exciting clash of primary colors. The islands jutted up, as if a huge flood had suddenly swept a range of mountains into existence. The waters seemed a sea within a forest, and the sun struck the surface with incredible brilliance.

Nearing the island, he ignored fundamental boating advice and stood up, surveying the shore for a suitable landing spot. He paralleled a line of cliffs, until a beach came into view. Then he dragged the boat up as far as he could, and tossed out the anchor onto the sand—just in case.

The only path led directly into a thicket. Scott pushed through, the lush undergrowth brushing against him, his feet crunching fallen twigs and leaves. He began to pant as he scaled a hill, flopping down at the crest, inhaling the pleasant evergreen aroma. A distant squawk of a bird broke the silence. Inland, the woods grew thicker; he turned in a wide circle back toward the water. Once satisfied that he was not lost, he began to skirt the water's edge. A hunger pain gnawed; he had not come well prepared. A new sound attracted his attention. He stopped walking, head alertly cocked.

Thwack, thwack, came the noises, evenly spaced. Scott

advanced, momentarily forgetting his stomach. *Thwack*. It was louder this time. He picked up the pace.

He stopped in a grove of trees at the top of a low hill, stationing himself under a protective canopy of branches. A stretch of beach, strewn with drifting wood logs, lay before him. The protesting creak of an ax being yanked out of wood followed each *thwack*. The woodsman stopped, turned toward Scott long enough to reveal his identity, mopped his brow, and resumed swinging.

Scott considered various strategies before pulling a harmonica from his pocket and blowing on it, not too loudly. *Thwack*, creak, *thwack*, creak, continued the cutting. Scott filled his lungs and sent a keening cluster of notes into the air. Greg's head swiveled like radar. He located the source. Scott watched him dig the ax into the log, stand motionless for an instant, still looking at him, then hoist his arms in a mock gesture of surrender, followed by a motion to come forward. Greg stayed where he was; Scott came to him.

His ragged beard could have been thicker, but Greg looked the part of a reclusive woodsman. He appeared much older, harder, and heavier than Scott remembered. His hair curled up from under his blue stocking cap. Greg broke the initial awkward silence.

"How did you know where to look?" His tone indicated that he suspected someone of betraying him. Scott considered several possible answers.

"Telepathy," he said.

They started into the bush, Scott assuming in the direction of some sort of lodging. Greg, who insisted on carrying the wood himself, stopped at one point, turned, and addressed Scott in clipped syllables, his jaw firm.

"I never let anyone come here."

Uncertain how to take this, Scott continued on with no reply, taking care to avoid the odd branch that Greg let fling back Inadvertently. They came to a clearing where Greg had assembled a dwelling neither tent nor cabin. It appeared to have been built in a hurry, or at night, almost nomadic, ready to be disassembled, thrown on a beast and carted off with a caravan. A carved eagle sat atop one of the poles, wooden wings spread wide. Taking in the scene, Scott rejected a remark about the place reminding him of a refugee camp with a view. He wanted to be as careful as possible with his brother.

"Should I take my shoes off?" he ventured.

Greg answered the biblical allusion with a cynical glance.

"Well," Scott continued, "I see you got the basic hut kit I sent you." He had been at the point of saying *hovel* instead of *hut.*

Greg seemed neither amused nor offended at Scott's assessment of his architectural prowess. He dumped the firewood in a heap, turned away, and gave a short whistle. Scott expected some toothy dog to come charging out, leap on him, and inundate his face, but that didn't happen.

"I'm coming," came a female voice after a few seconds.

A pretty, Nordic-looking girl emerged from behind the hut. Her light hair and skin sharply contrasted with the dark hues of the woods, as well as with her hairy companion. She appeared slightly puzzled about their impromptu visitor, but managed a smile.

"Miss Ursula Karlson. This is my brother, Scott Stuart."

Scott marked the lilt in her voice as she greeted him. Greg's spirits appeared to brighten.

"I had her sent over from Sweden."

"That's not true," Ursula protested with a slight pout.

"No. Actually, I met her at the island store. I think we were both reaching for the wheat germ."

Scott looked at the two of them. Greg could have passed for a longshoreman, while Ursula sported the latest wilderness high fashion, albeit slightly wrinkled. Near the door of the hut lay her blue nylon backpack, 35 millimeter camera, and expensive suede hiking boots, which she had temporarily forsaken for a pair of Adidas jogging shoes.

"I've always wanted to see Sweden," Scott said, making conversation.

"Oh, you must come," she replied. "Our house is always open."

The corners of Greg's eyes crinkled in a sly grin.

"Scott here," he said, sounding slightly professorial, is in his first year of seminary. They have those in Sweden, don't they?"

Ursula's expression grew quizzical. "You study religion?"

Scott laughed easily. "Why? Are you shocked?"

"This one," continued Greg, and gesturing to Scott, "has chained himself :o the mysteries of God. Personally, I'm convinced it had something to do with Sherlock Holmes in the sixth grade."

Scott tactfully avoided being baited into an argument. He asked Ursula about her family and travels, chuckling at the way she sometimes fouled up her English syntax. "My parents are playing always cards," she told him. He liked the rhythm of her voice. Their conversation drifted into trivialities, until Scott picked up a dogeared paperback with a drawing of a man reposing by a pond on the cover.

"Walden, huh?" said Scott, opening the volume, surprised to see some passages underlined.

"I've got to have something to read in the mornings. No sports section out here."

Scott barely restrained himself from telling Greg that, in his current decor, he appeared as distant from his earlier athletic enthusiasms as humanly possible. It was as though Jimmy Connors had opted for a career as a teamster. Greg took the volume from Scott and leafed through it.

"There is some good stuff in this. Helps me appreciate the island."

"I've always liked it, too," returned Scott. "Have you read it, Ursula?"

"No, but Greg is reading me always his favorite parts."

"Really?" said Scott, regarding Greg with approval.

"I feel like Walden's a neighbor. He seems to articulate how I feel living out here." Greg stopped turning the pages. "For example, sometimes you feel kind of cut off, like a hermit, then you stumble onto something like this."

He flipped pages, looking for a passage, then began to read in a voice that Scott thought bordered on being ministerial.

We are, for the most part, more lonely when we go abroad among men than when we stay in our chambers.

A choir of birds chirped in the background. It occurred to Scott to ask Greg if he had memorized the chapter and verse. Ursula appeared to sense that Scott wanted to speak with Greg alone and asked if she should go for a walk.

"No, no," protested Greg. "You can stay here in the condo. I want to show the Reverend Stuart the grounds."

Greg pulled Ursula close to him and kissed her. "We'll be back in a while."

"Wait a minute," Scott said. "Have you got anything to eat around here? All I've had since breakfast is a danish and a sandwich I bought at that stand where the ferry docks."

"Man, you are brave. Better hope you don't get trench-mouth."

Scott laughed, and Greg opened a cooler.

"What do you want? Take a pick."

Scott made his choice. "By the way, the old guy at the store says you're not supposed to be out there this time of year."

"You can tell him to ..." Greg looked around, assured himself that Ursula was out of range, then supplied Scott with a terse and unrepeatable statement to deliver to the old gentleman.

Scott munched on a granola bar as they walked down to the water's edge, where they ambled along, hurling driftwood logs and skipping stones.

"So how's it going in school?"

"Hey, they really pour it on. You know, homework on stone tablets."

Greg laughed and affected a Scottish brogue in his reply.

"So, who did you get for a rrroommate? Saint Frrrrrancis or Augustine?"

"Neither. The dorms were all booked."

"Oh, that must have made Mom happy. Keep you safe at home for a few more years."

"I'm not living at home. I took a third floor walk-up—Factorytown."

Greg stopped walking and looked at his brother as if he had just confessed an arrest for shoplifting.

"Factorytown? You're kidding? That . . ." Greg appeared to be searching for the right word. "That dump?"

Scott nodded. "Been there a couple months."

Still incredulous, Greg switched quickly to a jive dialect. "Do dey give you extra credits fo' *filth*, man?"

Scott lunged at him. "You redneck!" Greg ran off, laughing. Scott chased him, feet churning in the smooth stones. Greg slipped, cutting around a log too fast, enabling Scott to catch him. "Touchdown!" hollered Greg, holding up his hands, then making a motion of throwing down a football. The two celebrated the phantom score with a high five. Greg turned inland.

Scott wondered where they were going, but did not ask. Several times it occurred to him that life on the island might not be all that bad. It was unspoiled, pristine, and, unlike his apartment, quiet.

"How do you scrape up loose change around here?"

"Ursula came with a wad a travelers' checks."

"Oh, sorry I asked."

Greg, bristling at the implication he sponged off someone, stopped momentarily.

"No, I work. I work on the fishing boats out of Anacortes, when they need an extra body. You can bring in a couple hundred bucks if the catch is heavy."

"You like life out on the high seas, mate?" said Scott in an improvised cockney accent. They started walking again.

"Well, the money's good but they treat you like . . ." Looking at his seminarian brother, Greg changed the crude terms he was about to use, substituting, "Like a side of beef with a head." They passed along a worn path into a small clearing.

"So," Greg continued his statement, assuming his professorial manner again, "feeling the need to diversify, I've managed a small, supplemental stipend from my plantation."

A bevy of healthy marijuana plants surrounded them.

"Someone told me that stuff doesn't grow well up here."

"They lied," said Greg, lighting a rather large joint and taking a long toke. "Agriculture can be profitable. It sure beats slogging around in fish guts."

They sat down. Scott shook his head when the joint was extended his way. Greg took another toke; a seed popped. He appeared momentarily reflective, affable. Scott sensed this to be his best opportunity.

"Mom asked me to find you . . . She wants us home . . . for Dad's birthday."

"Dad's birthday?" he said, his tone implying, Is that all? "You mean this whole visit is a kind of singing telegram?"

When Scott did not reply, Greg seemed to regret the harshness of his statement.

"Man," he said quietly, "I am not the present he wants." Greg skillfully squeezed the burning end out of the joint and pocketed the rest for future reference. "How is Mom?"

"Distracted . . . distant. You know Mom."

Greg looked at Scott as if expecting further comment.

"I think I may have heard a faint S-O-S," Scott added, after a pause, as Greg stared at the ground near his feet. He stepped on the burning ash as they got up to leave.

On the way to the hut, Scott cleverly interwove their small talk with soft-sell appeals, planting several phrases he hoped would pierce Greg's armor, when he thought about them in solitude. The best of these were careful allusions to the condition of their mother. Near the clearing, pleasant smells wafted through the trees. Ursula, looking almost domestic, had begun to prepare a meal. Scott checked his watch; it was time he headed back. He declined to stay and eat, but accepted another granola bar.

Bidding good-bye to the couple and their makeshift homestead, Scott had to fight off a stab of envy. *Ostensibly,* he thought, *Greg has it made.* He looked at ease, at home, standing there beside Ursula, their little dwelling embowered in towering firs.

"I am happy to meet you, Scott," said Ursula, shaking his hand.

"Watch out for Bigfoot on the way back. You never know around here."

"I'll be on guard," said Scott, holding back on a final request for Greg to return home. He wished them well and struck out alone, finding the boat just as he had left it. The motor started on the second pull. He rode full throttle all the way, the little craft leaping and slapping the water.

On the ferry, Scott stayed in his car, reading from a Pocket Testament, thinking. He wondered if he had couched his appeal in the most effective way, and if he should have said more. The drive home seemed unduly long. He passed the muffler shop where he wanted to have the car fixed. It had closed for the day. In a phone booth, he dialed his mother, who had just come in from jogging.

"I found him," he said.

Anne was excited and happy and surprised. She questioned Scott in breathless spurts.

4

All morning the pain in his stomach had bothered him. It seemed to be spreading outwards, sapping his strength. Greg worked the deck with Tony, the only other hand.

The ancient vessel, inappropriately named *Faithful*, had long been ready for scrap. It listed badly to one side, its exterior rusty; underside barnacle-laden; its gear and tackle in disrepair; the nets a disgrace. Greg imagined it someday sinking to the bottom, and the great deep vomiting it up onto land in utter rejection. And yet, by some near miracle, it could still bring in a catch.

The old Chrysler gasoline engine alternately roared or stalled. When the latter occurred, the captain would rush over with a look of such rage that Greg fully expected him to grab the sixteen-pound sledge and bash the relic into fragments. The captain would swear at it for a minute or so without repeating himself, then somehow get it going again. He was a grizzled, gaunt man with awkward, jerky motions.

When he addressed Greg, his eyes looked disconcertingly off a few degrees. He had a strange, schizophrenic sort of manner, and Greg suspected that he was not "all there." Alternately, he stood on deck as if on a pleasure cruise, smoking a pipe, drinking whiskey, and talking to himself; or, he would rail against his crew with hostile fury, seldom pitching in with the work. He had been staring at Greg for some time. Greg could feel the eyes on him, unwelcome, because his own movements dragged. He feared he might be sick. The captain fled mercifully into the head.

"You're giving Cap the itch," said Tony, digging Greg with an elbow.

"Feeling's mutual," he shot back.

Greg often thought Tony a prototype deckhand: glib, combative, a descendant of fishermen, possessing potential for few other lines of work. He would sing along with gusto to pop songs, embarassingly off-key. When not so occupied, he would talk of the intricacies of fishing, as if they were skills mastered only by a select few. Still, Greg had learned a lot from him, laughed at his bawdy jokes, and found in him a valuable ally in dealing with such unpredictable types as Cap.

Tony, like many fishermen, talked about someday owning his own boat. Greg looked from Tony to Cap, visualizing the stages of evolution from one to the other. The single life and nightly partying into maybe his mid twenties. Then marriage, a growing family, thinner hair, thicker midsection, and harder work. Then, perhaps, his own boat, followed by years of boom and bust, each taking its toll physically, emotionally—until at last he stood, a replica of Cap, proud master of another floating junk pile. Greg could see it happening, and knew it was not for him. The pain in his stomach gnawed at him. He and Tony began to pull in the nets, bulging with fish.

"The problem is," said Tony after a long, uncharacteristic break of silence, "Cap ain't sure about you."

Greg listened but took care to keep working. He thought Tony might have a few doubts himself.

"You're a college type," Tony shrugged. "Maybe the IRS

checkin' him out?"

"Terrific," said Greg between his teeth, refuting the ridiculous notion with a sarcastic look.

"Hey, relax, man. Be cool. Think money."

Cap began to hover on deck, watching the two of them drag in a net of fish. Greg felt slightly dizzy; Tony, as if sensing this, appeared to work harder to compensate and cover for him. Greg felt the eyes bore into him again, this time accompanied by a raspy voice.

"Hey, kid, you puke on the deck, you clean it up yourself."

The fish flopping on the slick, wet deck made a sound like a hundred faces being slapped. Gulls flew reconnaissance for scraps of food. The captain, as if satisfied with delivering an edict on seasickness, retired to the cabin. Greg worked better in his absence, but the labor grew tedious, and he felt chilled. He wished he were back in his shanty, wrapped up snug in a sleeping bag with Ursula.

"You see," began Tony, his voice betraying an attitude of superiority in matters relating to fishing, "your problem is that you don't get to know 'em personally." He picked up a wriggling salmon from the deck and coddled it like an infant. "I mean take this one. I mean look at her—she's beautiful!"

Laughing, Tony thrust the fish into Greg's face.

"C'mon, give her a kiss. C'mon, c'mon, give her a kiss."

Greg retreated, parrying with his arms. He bumped into the guard rail and tumbled into the hold, the noise of his fall alerting Cap, who arrived at a gallop.

"He's stompin' the fish!" he yelled, glazed eyes flashing.

Greg, unhurt by the fall, regained his footing. *Stomping the fish? This was a sin*, he reflected, *of which he had hitherto heard nothing, though he had made almost every other mistake in his brief fishing career.*

"He's trouble." Cap said to Tony. "He cost me! That college puke cost me! No full share! No way!"

Greg was relieved to hear Tony go to bat for him.

"Hey, Cap, c'mon. We had a good set. Almost fifteen

hundred pounds! He earned it."

"He's stompin' the fish, guinea!" repeated Cap, pointing insanely at the hold, finger trembling. Tony turned on him.

"Hey, who you callin' *guinea*, dog breath? You wanna lose your crew? He doesn't get his full share, I walk!"

Cap, evidently not popular with fishermen, appeared to see an elementary logic in this. "He's trouble," he repeated, looking off to one side. Everything on the boat seemed to be creaking and moaning. The radio crackled with static. Cap went inside to answer. Tony, voice echoing, hoisted Greg out of the hold.

"You gotta know how to talk to Cap in a way he understands. He's missing a few dots off his dice anyway."

"Thanks, Tony. I owe you one."

Tony made a stereotypical Italianized gesture. "Hey, Mr. IRS, we're *compares*, right?"

"Right," he said, without understanding, exactly, what *compares* meant.

Heading in, Greg wanted to avoid the usual experience of having Tony talk at him. He took out *Walden*, even though he felt little inclination to read. Tony tolerated the situation only so long.

"Hey, whatcha got here?" He snatched the book from Greg (evidently expecting a hot pocket novel), and was disappointed not to see a panting vixen on the cover. "Walden? Whatsit about? Any good parts in it?"

Greg summarized the book in simple terms.

"Kinda like what you're doin', huh?"

"I guess, in a way."

Greg had not really been reading, just holding the book as a way of keeping silence. His eyes fell on a passage. When Tony finally left him alone, he read it.

Most men, even in this comparatively free country, through mere ignorance and mistake, are so occupied with the factitious cares and superflously coarse labors of life that its finer fruits cannot be plucked by them. Their fingers, from excessive toil, are too clumsy and tremble too much for that. Actually, the laboring man has not leisure for a true integrity day by day . . . he has no time to be anything but a machine.

No time to be anything but a machine. The phrase stuck with him all the way back. He watched the boat's wake unzip the water's surface. It had almost an hypnotic effect on him.

The *Faithful* docked at Anacortes, its engine running on after being shut off. Following his custom, Cap shrieked at it, and as if in reluctant obedience, the old power plant shook to a stop with a noisy, gassy-smelling belch through the carburetor, kind of a last act of defiance.

"Thanks for sticking up for me," Greg told Tony, as they collected their money.

"Remember," he returned with a wink, "you owe me one."

Greg thought Tony had slim chance of ever collecting.

It was getting dark by the time Greg made it back to the island. He caught a welcome whiff of frying food a long way off, wondering what process or instincts possessed Ursula to have everything ready for him each time he returned from work. She had braided her hair, and looked like a blond Indian.

"I wouldn't get too close," cautioned Greg. "I must smell like a ton of fish."

He stretched out on a blanket; his whole body throbbed. He nearly drifted off to sleep.

"Greg, you are eating?"

Hunger overruling his fatigue, he ate a helping, unable to let Ursula go to all the trouble for nothing. She boiled water for coffee. Everything consumed and cleaned up, she plunked herself down in his lap and held his face between her hands. Smoke from the fire looped up. The night air held a chill breath. Stars shone through the trees, unhindered by lesser lights. They joined in a long, leisurely kiss. When they broke, Greg gave a short chuckle that Ursula appeared to misunderstand. She looked at him as he shook his head and began a slow giggle. Soon they were both laughing. He explained his reservations about the working life. How even the fish seemed just so much bulk fodder —smelly hunks of protein— different creatures from the shimmering beauties caught by sportsmen and held up for admiration. Ursula sympathized with him. Later, they got into a complicated discussion about philosophy. She had a tendency to quote from films by Ingmar Bergman and Lina Wertmuller. Greg had never heard of the latter. They both eventually fell asleep by the fire. Greg's last conscious thought was that there would be no fishing for him tomorrow. He dreamed of enormous salmon, mouths gaping, rushing toward his face, forcing him backwards, till he fell in a hold where an echoing cry of "He's stompin' the fish!" rang in his ears. He saw himself as an old hunched-over salt dog, with a salt and pepper beard and gnarled hands. The vision woke him up.

He rose early and walked down to the water's edge. The day greeted him with a kind of scowl. The overcast sky and agitated waters fueled his feeling of uneasiness. Returning to the hut, he started on the chapter of *Walden* titled "Conclusion." He had been so taken with the details of Thoreau's sojourn in the wilds, that he had almost forgotten that the writer had not stayed there permanently.

Ursula slept longer than usual. She wiggled out of her sleeping bag and playfully chided Greg for not putting on the water for coffee (to which she seemed addicted). Making the preparations herself, she realized that Greg was struggling with something. She planted a light kiss on his cheek. He expected her to ask if he was still too tired, or some other seductive phrase, but she said:

"How is your reading?"

"Do you really want to know?"

She nodded. He turned back a page and read to her:

I left the woods for as good a reason as I went there. Perhaps it seemed to me that I had several more lives to live, and could not spare any more time for that one.

She looked at him, a wistful sadness in her expression. Wisps of hair had broken free from her braids and played across her face. She requested no further explanations. None were necessary.

5

S cott read the sentences for the fourth time:

"All proponents of heterodox Deutero-Isaiah theories and arbitrary documentary hypotheses, such as those stridently advanced by Wellhausen and others, exhibit a marked tendency to disregard "chiliasm" (a pejorative designation) in its entirety, even in its transcendental dimension; thus revealing clearly a hermeneutic deriving from antisupernatural presuppositions. Even Reformed theologians . . .

He stopped. What Reformed or unreformed theologians thought of this Scott did not care; he could not make head or tail out of it. He had been buried in books all day, wading through volumes of systematic theology, New Testament Greek, hermeneutics, ethics, and other subjects. It occasionally occurred to him that a conspiracy might exist among theologians to avoid a clearly stated sentence. Latin, Greek, or German footnotes in the text often seemed to him as frivolous gamesmanship, upper-story scholars with powerful minds, writing only for each other. Scott studied the material, learned it, and regurgitated it on papers and in exams, but doubted if a large part of it had much to do with everyday life in places like Factorytown.

Certainly looking around his dingy apartment did nothing to help his concentration. The walls, painted a "summer complaint" yellow, were peeling and cracked. A few posters covered the worst of the holes left by previous tenants. The Early Goodwill Industries decor was evident in the sagging couch; one equally sagging overstuffed chair; an orange crate coffee table; a few metal folding chairs; an old bridge lamp; and one shadeless table lamp, resting uncomfortably on another orange crate, this one standing on end. A small area rug made of indeterminate materials covered part of the wide floor boards. His desk from home was the only reminder of his Capitol Hill origins.

Stopping to rest his eyes, he discovered a strong desire to watch any mindless nonsense. "I Love Lucy," "Gilligan's Island" reruns—anything, however fatuous—as a kind of mental cathartic; but he had shunned television as part of the experiment in what his fellow students in the Poverty Project called simple living. He tried reading an article about the various Christian views of poverty in *Sojourners* magazine, but the baleful graphics of the publication depressed him. He got up and turned the clock so he couldn't see it, ate an apple, straightened up a few things in the generally untidy room, then got back down to work. The kitchen faucet dripped. Noises came from outside. Scott could feel the vibrations through the old walls. He tried valiantly for five minutes to carry on studying, but the pounding continued. He shut the books and opened the door to the third floor porch.

A black boy, about eight, dribbled a basketball on the open porch, faking and driving by imaginary opponents like a miniature Kareem Abdul Jabbar or Julius Erving. His raggedy clothes fit him poorly; the laces on one of his shoes were undone; he had some crusted food around the corners of his mouth.

"Hi."

A siren sounded a few streets over. A dog barked. The lad tried to spin the ball on his index finger but it rolled off. He looked Scott up and down, wary of him.

"How you doing?"

"Fine." The boy managed a weak smile.

"You . . . here all by yourself?"

"My mom works at the hospital. I'm waiting for her to come home.

"I'm Scott."

"Man, you got a lot of books in there," peering through the window.

"Yes." He knew the ice was broken. "I'm going to this really tough school."

"Why?" queried the boy, thumping the ball again. "Do they make you?"

This wrung a laugh out of Scott, and a memory of how he had once regarded school himself.

"No, I'm going because I want to."

The concept did not sit well with the boy. "Man, you're weird."

"What's your name?"

"Oliver Robinson. My mom calls me Oliver, but I like Ollie."

"Want to shoot a few, Ollie?"

Oliver thought a minute. "Okay."

"You sure it's all right?"

"Uh-huh. It's okay."

They walked to a schoolyard court, where Scott missed his first three shots, blaming the rim, bent from the effects of neighborhood slam dunk artists hanging on it.

"Doctor Airball!" he proclaimed himself, putting up a shot that missed by a yard.

He let Oliver shoot and retrieved the ball for him, lavishing the boy with compliments on his skill. A series of screams came from an adjoining lot.

Two youths attempted to tear the purse away from a young woman who fiercely resisted. She tumbled to the ground in the struggle. Scott tossed the ball aside and instinctively ran toward her; the assailants fled as he approached. He helped her up, comforting. She looked vaguely familiar, but out of place among the old houses and buildings of that part of Seattle, as though a young lady from his parents' area had gotten lost, returning home from shopping.

"One of the many things I love about living in this neighborhood," she told him.

Oliver had retrieved the ball and looked on without comment.

"Are you sure you didn't lose anything?"

"No, I think I've got everything, thank you." Her voice was clear and calm.

Scott thought she looked at him an inordinately long time. He began to wonder what she would say.

"Are you Scott Stuart?" It was half a question.

Genuinely surprised, Scott hesitated before answering. He hadn't really appraised her; she was pretty, in a natural, wholesome sort of way, with a disarming smile. Her plain, functional clothing did not emphasize her best features, a fact Scott noticed immediately.

"Yes. How did you know?" he added, not caring about the answer.

"Well, I heard you were living here—I saw your name on the Poverty Project list at school."

He started to say something. She gestured to her left.

"I live just around the corner."

Scott explained where he lived. "This is my friend, Oliver. He lives next door."

"Hello, Oliver."

Oliver dribbled back to the court and neatly sank a layup.

"You didn't say what your name was."

"Oh, I'm sorry. I'm Laura. Laura Jaffe."

"Well," he began clumsily, "that's great. We'll have to, uh, get together and ..."

She smiled and finished his sentence.

"... exchange Factorytown notes."

He accompanied her to the point where he and Oliver had to turn off. Insults had been sprayed on a wall in huge block letters.

"Lock your door."

"I will. You, too."

Oliver asked, "She your girl?" eliciting a casual laugh.

On the way home, Scott debated what to do about Oliver. It did not seem right to leave him by himself, unattended. *On the other hand,* he thought, *he did have some serious studying to do.* A look at the pompous volume full of unreadable prose awaiting him tipped the scales. Scott was torn between his mountain of homework and his commitment to be available to his neighbors.

"You have anything else to do, Oliver?"

He shook his head.

"You want to come in for a while? I've got some things we can do—if your mother won't mind."

Ollie came into Scott's flat without hesitation, immediately running his hands along the rows of books he had previously observed through the porch window. The sheer size of the Systematic Theology text seemed to impress him.

"Have you read this whole thing?"

"Read it?" said Scott. "I haven't even weighed it. Here, Ollie, sit down a minute."

The spartan apartment did not offer much in the way of facilities. "I know what we can do."

Scott gathered some bars of soap and a pair of kitchen knives. The two of them sat there, littering the floor, as Scott guided Oliver in making a soap rowboat. He finished one himself and left it with the lad for a model. Then he started typing up an outline for a paper due the following Friday. Oliver worked away in silence. Scot heard the steps creak.

"Oliver?" came a voice from outside.

"Oliver!" A door opened and shut. Scott could hear her

pacing around outside.

"Where are you?! You get your tail in here this minute! You hear?"

Scott swallowed, composing lines of explanation.

"I'm in here, Mom," Ollie said as Scott opened the door.

"Excuse me, Mrs. Robinson. I'm Scott Stuart." He tried to sound diplomatic. She ignored him and drew a bead on Oliver, hands on her hips.

"How many times do I have to tell you to stay at home?"

Oliver held up a boat made of soap, and a rough pair of soap-sculptured oars to go with it. "Look at the things I made, Mom."

She appeared ready to tongue-lash him again, but stopped. "Well, now," she said, picking up the boat, then handing it back, "that is something."

"See all those books," he said, pointing. "He reads 'em."

"What do you think you do with books? You hush a minute now."

Mrs. Robinson turned to Scott. She was a handsome woman —he guessed about thirty-four—erect and dignified, but with worry lines around the eyes, the whites of which were cracked with red lines. The light nurse's aide uniform made her seem very dark. She addressed Scott in a slightly different tone than what she had used with her son, but still edged with displeasure.

"Are you from this area? You don't look like it, if you don't mind me saying so."

"No, I'm afraid I'm not from this area. At least not originally."

"And where are you from, 'originally'?"

"I grew up in Capitol Hill."

Her eyes widened. "*Capitol Hill?* What do you want to come and live in a toilet like this for?" She paused, eyes narrowing. "You in some kind of trouble?"

"No. I don't think so," he said. "I go to Northwest Seminary." He forced a smile. "I guess that explains all the books."

The word *seminary* had tripped something. "Dear God,"

she said, and pulling Oliver close, "are you one of those Moonies?"

The term drew an involuntary laugh from Scott. He thought her guard might be dropping. The ends of her mouth made an effort at an upward turn. Then the debris Oliver had left on the floor caught her attention.

"Oliver, I swear, child, you're a mess looking for a place to happen. Now you clean it up, right now."

"It's all right, Mrs. Robinson. I'll clean it up later."

"Run along home, then. I'll be right there."

Oliver left, stepping in the soap shavings, flattening them out on the rug. Scott managed to coax Mrs. Robinson into sitting down.

"Excuse me for being so blunt, but it doesn't look good for a little boy to be in a strange apartment. Not the way things are with all these perverts around."

"I understand. Oliver was bouncing the ball outside on the porch. I saw him all alone, and we went and shot some baskets. Then I thought he might want to . . . excuse me, is there something wrong?"

Mrs. Robinson had bowed her head and covered her eyes with a hand. He thought he heard her say something to herself. She shook her head and coughed. "No, no, nothing."

"I just thought I might be able to give him something to do."

"Thank you. You're sure you're not involved in one of these cults?"

Scott sensed she knew the answer. "No, I'm just a Christian."

Her tired, pained expression gave way to one Scott thought bordered on bafflement.

"You know, sometimes I don't understand." She let out a sigh. "I've been working and pleading with God for years to get me out of this place. Now a white boy from Capitol Hill wants to move in. I don't understand some people."

Scott said, "Let me try and explain."

He told her that he and other Northwest Seminary students were part of a program to live in areas where they might be able to help their neighbors—a sort of Christianity-in-action.

"Oh, I see," said Mrs. Robinson unconvincingly.

6

The very house in which he had grown up, the only house he had ever lived in, was to Scott atypical in the eighties. He stood, looking at the massive two-story dwelling, standing in its amphitheatre of trees. *It might have been a hotel*, he thought, noting the four white columns bracketing the porch, and the two-tiered brick steps leading to the ornate oak door with its circular window. The hedges, shrubs, and grass had, as usual, been carefully and professionally manicured. The interior was likewise immaculate, the product of his mother's tastes for eighteenth-century English antiques. In front of all this, his tired blue car looked out of place, and, searching inward, he felt that way himself.

The Reverend Keith Wharton and his wife had arrived before him, special guests for Elton's birthday dinner. Anne set five places. The minister at Elton's request, said grace.

"... and a special blessing on thy servant Elton, on this, his birthday. *Amen.*

Scott, with some difficulty, took care not to pile too much

food on his plate, to avoid giving his parents the impression that the meals he cooked himself might be less than adequate—something he knew to be completely true. His mother had prepared a banquet. Reverend Wharton addressed Scott as he passed the potatoes.

"How is school going, Scott?"

"I'd have to say that it hasn't been easy, but I seem to manage."

"We had heard," the minister continued, choosing his words, "that you were living in the industrial section—what they call Factorytown, I believe."

"Doesn't it conflict with your studies?" Mrs. Wharton quickly added.

Scott tried to visualize the conversation that might have taken place before he arrived. "Not at all. In fact, I think mainstream Christianity is in a ghetto of its own and I'm not comfortable with that."

Scott felt himself a kind of target.

"But, aren't there people who work down there?" his mother asked.

"Mom, you know that's not an argument."

"I just mean that ... that there are agencies ..."

"A lot of this poverty talk," interjected Elton, bunching up his napkin and wiping his mouth, "strikes me as the latest fad. I think it is all a bit ostentatious. 'I'm more working class than you, and I'm going to make sure everybody knows about it.' To be totally honest, the whole idea strikes me as a kind of reverse snobbery."

Rev. Wharton had been poised to say something all through Elton's speech. "I would grant that there is a danger of reverse snobbery and attitudes of that sort, but I think, in Scott's case, it might be some distant revivalist ancestor surfacing."

"Of course, we're thrilled with Scott's dedication," Anne began, but—a horrible noise, the squealing of tires, caused her to stop. Necks craned toward the window.

"Hey, it's Greg!" Scott announced.

"Scott, please, set a place for him." Anne didn't want Greg to realize they hadn't expected him.

In the driveway, Greg dismounted a snorting, old, Triumph Bonneville. He lugged a backpack to the front door, where Elton greeted him.

"I made it," Greg said, without a lot of emotion. "Happy birthday."

"Good to see you, son."

Greg deposited his heavy coat and backpack in the hall. Elton wrinkled his nose.

"Am I imagining things, or do I smell fish?"

"The coat, probably. I was out on a trawler last week. You want me to go upstairs and change?"

Elton put a hand on his son's shoulder. "No, no, no! We're all here, waiting for you."

Greg spoke little during dinner other than to request the passing of another dish. He consumed a huge quantity of food, eating on long after the others had finished.

"How is it going for you on your own, Greg?" queried Rev. Wharton.

"Is 'fantastic' too strong?" He modified this with, "Fine, actually."

"Your beard is ... striking."

"Thank you. I hate shaving."

"And you look fit as well."

Anne turned to Mrs. Wharton. "Well ... we haven't heard anything about your trip to the Holy Land. Greg, the Whartons were there just last month. Tell us, how was it?"

It appeared to be a favorite subject with the lady.

Well, we didn't stay too long in Jerusalem. It is so crowded; you have to see it to believe it. And, quite frankly, I was just a little bit nervous with all this terrorist business and so forth. You keep thinking one of the PLO people might toss a grenade right into one of the tourist buses. I prefer the countryside, much more serene. The trouble is, everything is so commercialized. Keith ... oh, it was such a surprise! He insisted on a boat ride on the Sea of Galilee. You wouldn't believe the prices, Anne. Outrageously expensive!"

Greg looked up from his plate, mouth full, and said, "Maybe that's why Jesus walked?"

Scott let a laugh escape, then held back, stifling the impulse. Elton looked pained. Anne turned red. Mrs. Wharton's eyebrows had raised. Her husband just looked blank, as if trying to decide what to say. Greg, oblivious to the reactions, chewed on without interruption.

They moved into the living room, where Anne served coffee and after-dinner mints. Elton stoked up a fire and sat in his favorite chair. The others looked on, as he unwrapped a present.

"Oh, I've always wanted one of these."

He held up a sleek, designer attache case.

"Trouble is, I could never bring myself to get rid of the old one. Kind of like a favorite pair of pants. Thank you all very much."

Greg had gone into the hall and fetched something out of his backpack. He walked over to Elton, offered him a small wooden carving of a porpoise. The piece had not been finely detailed, but possessed a certain rustic charm, enhanced by the thick varnish. Elton was obviously moved.

"Is this your work?" he asked, and Greg nodded. Elton groped for the right words to express his appreciation, not only for the gift but for the artistry.

"Thank you, son. I ... I ... don't know what to say to tell you how much this means to me. I'm going to keep this right here on the mantle." He placed it between two of Greg's tennis trophies. "Thank you very much, son."

Greg was pleased and touched at his father's obvious pleasure.

Later in the evening Scott monitored Greg's fascination with his old tennis awards. It seemed as if that whole dimension of his life were a new discovery, a wistful projection, and not history. He compared himself with a picture a couple of years old, taken on the court after a tournament victory.

"The same guy?" Scott asked.

Greg thought a moment. "What does anybody have in common with an old picture, other than they happen to be the same person?"

"Is that from Thoreau?"

"No."

"By the way, what happened to Ursula?"

"She might be back in Uppsala by now. I put her on a bus for British Columbia. I think she has a relative there. She's going to fly back home."

The predominant odor in the room was one of fish.

"You know, these clothes of yours. Do you think you could stow them on the roof? Maybe let the night air work on them awhile?"

Greg quickly veered from his tennis nostalgia.

"Is that what you tell the lost souls down in Factorytown? 'Frankly, my man, your clothes stink. Try a night on the roof.' Must make quite an impression. Mine stink because I earned money working in them. I'm not a career student."

Greg walked out on a balcony, extracting another large joint, lighting it with a white lighter. He took a long toke in full view of Scott, who looked on with frowning disapproval.

"Greg, you're way out of line. If Dad gets a whiff of that, he'll ..."

"Oh, come on!" Greg took a quick hit. "Look, the birthday boy's got his vices, and I've got mine." He held up the joint, examining it closely, paraphrasing the Bible in a mock sanctimonious voice not unlike that of Rev. Wharton as he did so, "... and God saw every green herb bearing seed that he had created," he drew on the weed deeply, its red ember glowing brightly, "and loooooo," he blew out the smoke in the direction of Scott's face, "it was goooood!"

Scott pondered a way to refute this. "Put it out," he said. Greg, surprisingly, acquiesced with no debate on the evils, medical or moral, of *Cannabis sativa*.

"All right, I don't want to rain on the big evening."

He took a final toke before putting out the joint, saving the rest, as he had done on the island.

Scott persuaded Greg to play the guitar, while he accompanied on harmonica. In the middle of a rough twelve-bar blues, Elton knocked and walked in.

"Hi, Dad. Pull up a chair, and let us entertain you!"

Elton, stiff and nervous, declined, continuing to stand near the door. He turned his attention to Greg.

"Since it looks as if I'll only be seeing you possibly every few months, I guess I better ask any questions I have quickly ... well, it concerns us just what you are intending to do at this juncture of your life."

"Dad," returned Greg, setting down the guitar, "you have worried about me for twenty-one years, right? Listen, as of this moment, I am relieving you of the responsibility. Don't worry about it."

"You have to do more than just survive in this day and age, son. Why, any thinking person ..."

"I haven't been here three hours and already we're into an employment interview! Why is it always questions and decisions with you, Dad? Please, back off."

"Greg, if you can just show some control, I have something to say to you. Please hear me out." Elton's speech slowed, and mellowed. "Your mother heard there's an opening at the Ivygate Tennis Club. They are in the market for an instructor with good tournament credentials. You might want to check it out." He moved toward the door and looked back at both of them. "It's good to have both of you here. Good night."

"Happy birthday, Dad," said Scott.

The door closed. Greg twanged the strings of the guitar with one hand.

"Going to take a run at it?"

"I don't know. Fishing in the cold doesn't actually thrill me. Actually, any kind of fishing doesn't thrill me. I have this aversion to physical work." An idea struck him. "Why don't you implore the deity for your neopagan brother?"

"I do," Scott told him flatly. Greg flung a pillow at him.

"Man, you are a monk."

Scott found it hard to sleep in the silence of Capitol Hill. He had grown used to the noise of traffic, breaking bottles, and the domestic quarrels that filtered unedited into his apartment. In the morning he heard Greg fumbling in the closet, followed by the front door closing. Scott got up and trotted down the curved staircase. Seeing his mother looking out the window, he joined her there. Outside, Greg headed off at a brisk jog, racquets in hand. Scott looked at his mother. Her face wore an expression of pure joy.

7

"**W**hy should I hire you?"

Mr. Fredericks, the dapper manager of the Ivygate Tennis Club, had emphasized the *you* in his question. Another candidate for the job had arrived minutes before and stood by. Greg immediately thought, *Because I'm better than that wimp beside you, that's why,* but said: "Well, I'm not too ugly." He had shaved his bushy beard and had his hair cut.

The audacity of this seemed to impress the man. "How do you get along with people?"

"Fine."

"Ah, but can you teach? You see, we have a very discerning clientele. None of them pays for lessons with food stamps, if you understand my meaning. They achieve everywhere else, and they fully expect to achieve here. The man I hire obviously must be capable of guiding them to that end." He gestured to the other candidate. "Now, Jack, here, spent the entire summer at one of those hot-shot tennis camps in Maine."

Jack interjected, "Thirty-four outdoor, twelve indoor courts. An instructor for every four students. It was dynamite."

Greg groaned inwardly at the adolescent inflection of *It was dynamite*. He noticed that both Fredericks and Jack, a lanky, preppy type, wore shirts that he hated, the ones with a little alligator over the pocket. Jack wore an expression of fathomless arrogance.

"The question remains," continued Fredericks, "Why should I hire you?"

Well, why should he? Greg asked himself. Surveying the adjoining courts where some middle-aged ladies played, he pointed out one woman.

"That lady out there—the one with the visor. She's already looking downcourt before she makes contact. And her weight. It's all on the back foot. She doesn't step into the shot. No power. And you can see from here, her friend's using too much wrist." Turning back to Fredericks, Greg declared, "I could improve their games twenty- to twenty-five percent in one session."

Jack appeared ready to burst into laughter over the claim, but Fredericks was impressed. He sized both of them up, hand on his chin.

"Well, he said, "I guess I'll have to see you two on the court."

"You mean play for the job?"

"Yes." Fredericks seemed pleased with his own idea, and eager to see them fight it out.

"Now?"

"Why not?"

Greg knew full well that any explanation for not being in top form along the lines of, "Well, I've been living out on an island and working on trawlers and haven't been able to practice," would contradict things he had already said, and possibly default everything to his opponent. He tried to dredge up confidence.

"Why not?" Greg echoed. "Let's do it."

As they prepared for the match to be played on an outdoor court, Jack taunted him. "What tournaments did you
say you won?"

"I didn't."

"Call it."

Jack spun the racket, let it fall. The match began under a
bright noonday sun.

Greg surprised himself with his first serves. Chopping
wood and hauling fish had strengthened his upper body. The
serves packed a zip and a high-kicking bounce, but lacked
accuracy. Jack, discovering that Greg was not in top form, hit
from the baseline, forcing him all over the court, winning the
first set easily.

In the second, Jack began missing first serves. Finding
his legs, Greg started coming to the net, powering several
clean shots.

It was just about lunchtime, and men and women heading for the cocktail lounge, coffee shop, or restaurant hurried
over when they saw the spirited match. The olympic-size
pool emptied quickly, as excitement started to mount. Even
the "reading room," usually populated by the nonathletic
members (who had only joined the club because of its repu-
tation for catering to the wealthy and socially elite) was va-
cant as members hastened to the court where Jack and
Greg were battling it out.

So many people crowded around, that Fredericks
stopped the match at one point and called for silence. The
manager appeared to enjoy the proceedings, as if he were officiating the U.S. Open on national television, with McEnroe
and Borg as finalists. Greg's next point, a backhand volley at
the end of an exhausting rally, drew an *Ooh* from the crowd,
then scattered applause. Jack committed successive double
faults. Rattled, he went on to lose the second set 6-4 with numerous unforced errors.

Rediscovering a killer instinct and hoping to finish Jack
off in a hurry, Greg threw all his force into every shot, but
again became erratic, falling behind 3-4. Jack, now inundat-

ed with sweat, abandoned his big-serve strategy for the base-line tactics that had won him the first set, planning, Greg felt sure, to let his opponent beat himself. But Jack's baseline ground strokes, both backhand and forehand, had lost their sting. Greg felt loose and confident. He charged all over the court on search and destroy missions, bashing wicked, accurate missiles to alternating corners, delighting the crowd. A sporadic squealing noise distracted him as he prepared to serve. He searched for the source, as he mopped his brow with a forearm.

A woman in the crowd with long brown hair wielded a motor-driven Nikon, its telephoto lens fixed on him. She lowered the camera and met Greg's eyes for an instant.

"Quiet, please," intoned Fredericks.

Greg heard the Nikon whine all through his serve, which just ticked the line for his fourth ace. Jack glanced up at the chair, but did not argue. Greg battled his way into the lead, surprising even himself on some shots, particularly one two-handed screamer from deep in the corner that left Jack chopping at the air.

"Match point," droned Fredericks. The crowd responded with cheers. They had been on Greg's side since he came back from losing the first set. He now led 5-4, but Jack served and could force a tiebreaker by taking the game. Greg wanted to end it here. Both feet had blisters; his shirt stuck annoyingly to his body; one of his calf muscles felt cramped.

"Quiet, please. Quiet in the stands."

The crowd hushed to complete silence. Jack bounced the ball in his pre-serve ritual. The noise echoed. Greg played deep, expecting him to go for an ace, at least on his first try, but the ball approached with a slow, tantalizing bounce. Jack retreated in anticipation of a bullet return. Greg charged, checked his swing and cleverly chipped the ball into the opposite court. Caught hopelessly out of position, Jack ran in with a valiant lunge, sending his frame sprawling onto the court, and the ball dribbling into the net. The audience roared approval. Greg clenched his fists and leaped.

"Game, set and match to Mr. Stuart," Fredericks announced.

Greg felt pulses, rushes of exultation. Club members crowded around him, complimenting, congratulating, filling the air with glowing adjectives, imparting to him a sense of power. Women touched him on the arms. One bejewelled, faintly mustached matron gushed, "Oh, I'm just so thrilled you're going to be on staff here!"

"I think we have the right man," Fredericks told him, after waiting his turn to get near, pumping Greg's hand. "Your game reminds me of mine when I was your age."

In the parking lot, Greg experienced a shiver of pure delight at the sight of the vanquished Jack driving off in a Mercedes-Benz 450 SL with a personalized plate proclaiming PRO. He kicked the bike to life and drove triumphantly along Lake Washington in kind of a one-motorcycle procession, overwhelmed with what had happened. He continued as far as Yessler, where he turned and headed for home. Anne Stuart couldn't hear enough about the match.

"I really kicked his . . . I beat him bad," he told her.

The next day, after his first teaching session, he drove to his brother's to break the news personally. He was carrying with him the photographs the attractive brunette had taken of him during the match. She had deliverd them to him personally during the teaching session. He couldn't talk to her at length then, but he did find out that she was Sheila Holt-Browning, professional photographer. His student told him, "She's 'top drawer,' and her father's a big wheel in the U.S. Tennis Association." Greg was very interested.

Scott heard the rumble of the bike and bounded down the stairs, missing the step that creaked. Greg heralded the news as they walked up.

"Ah, the thrill of victory. I can see the headline," said Scott, "Thoreau Buff Bags Tennis Job."

Greg's laugh cackled. "How about 'Island Upstart Whomps Wimp?' You should of heard him," Greg went into an exaggerated imitation of Jack. "Thirty-four outdoor, twelve indoor. It was *dyyynamite!* Hey, I'll tell you, swinging that ax all summer really paid off. My serves were zinging in there like laser beams."

"High tech tennis, huh?"

"Really. If I could've gotten more serves in, I'd have really killed him. So, anyway, I'm in and fancy Jack's going back to his *dyyynamite* tennis camp. Anybody who wears one of those shirts with the little alligators over the pocket needs lessons."

Scott shook his head, grinning. They went inside the dingy flat.

"Wow," said Greg, looking around, recalling their conversation on the island. "I see you got the basic 'dump' kit I sent you. What is this decor? Wait, don't tell me. Uh, it's either Early Tacky or Contemporary Squalor, right?"

The place smelled of the old rag rug, stale bread and peanut butter. The drip from the kitchen faucet plunked into a pot blackened with burned rice. Scott had put up free Chamber of Commerce posters of Seattle, seen from the Space Needle and other vistas, but the place was downright depressing.

"It's . . . paid for."

"Dad been here yet?"

Scott shook his head.

"I guess a lot of folks on your block don't think too highly of hygiene."

"Greg, go easy now."

"You really feel this is where you are supposed to be?"

"Yes. I'd be happy to explain it all to you if you've got some time."

"Some other time, maybe. I should get back." He paused a moment. "You sure nobody will steal my bike out there?"

"I don't know why they'd want to."

Greg conceded the point and changed the subject. He produced a manila envelope full of black and white photos. "Look at these. Just like *Sports Illustrated.* Real pro job. Check out this one."

Scott examined the pictures, nodding agreement. "This one's the best." The shot showed Greg twisted like a corkscrew, poised to unleash a backhand, eyes trained on the ball frozen in flight, face taut with emotion. "Who had the camera on you?"

"Sheila Holt-Browning." Greg sounded as if announcing the entrance of royalty.

"A photographer and she's hyphenated?"

"The name sounds old, but only her money is. Her father's a wheel in the U.S.T.A. Of course that isn't the only thing about her that is interesting."

"I see."

"I think," said Greg in an attempted brogue, "that the lady has taken a fancy to me."

8

Reverend Keith Wharton arrived at church early, surprised to find Anne Stuart arranging flowers for the morning service, something that, to the best of his knowledge, she had not done for some time.

"Anne, those flowers are gorgeous. Thank you so much."

"Oh, hello, Keith . . . I mean Reverend—it doesn't seem right to call you Keith here." She looked at the flowers, touching a petal. "It seemed a shame not to share them."

He smiled at her. "I wish you'd call me Keith all the time. How's the family doing?"

"Fine. Greg's back at home. He got a job as a tennis instructor."

"Oh, Anne, that's great news!"

She shared details of the match, embellishing Greg's account the tinlest blt.

"When they ask me whose green thumb produced these beauties, may I tell them?"

64

"Just tell them," she said after a pause, "that they are from a very happy lady."

Retreating into his walnut-paneled study, the minister observed Anne sitting alone in a pew near the front, head bowed. The sun's slanting rays, breaking through a gray broom of rain, diffused the colors of the stained-glass windows throughout the rich interior. The sanctuary was a traditional one. A large oriental rug had been placed on the marble floor. The dark oak kneelers covered with deep red velvet were as solid as the congregation members they held. Everything in the church reflected the wealth, the good taste of its supporters.

Anne's seemed a wordless celebration. Rev. Wharton left her to her meditations and began his own with a long prayer.

He had always found it difficult to pray for Greg, ever since, some years earlier, Greg had flippantly asked him how it felt to "bore for the Lord," an insult that earned the full wrath of his father. The remark had often returned to the pastor, especially during sermons, when he stood staring at a solid phalanx of faces, many obviously less than enthralled with his performance, impassive as granite. *Had he ever forgiven the lad?* he asked himself, sending beams of light to search out a corner of his soul. Before God, he took care of the matter, then began to go over his notes.

The morning message dealt with the sixth chapter of Matthew, and Jesus' promise to provide all things to those who first sought the Kingdom of God. It was, he knew, a tricky theme for his affluent parishioners. Keith Wharton often thought how the twentieth century, including even some of Christ's ostensible followers, had managed to turn Jesus' words upside down: *cursed are those who weep, for they are imbalanced; blessed are the impure, for they shall be spared the sight of God; buy this in remembrance of me.* Wharton searched, prayed for *mots justes*, the right words to impart the message, but, too often, felt as if speaking into the air. He suspected, with reasonable justification, that during his talk, some would be pondering a sloop or vacation home, others juggling the Dow Jones averages or the Consumer Price Index; still others awaiting the end of his sermon with baited breath, worried about missing the opening kickoff of the Seahawk game. One consolation of the present age was that those openly hostile to his message seldom, if ever, darkened the door of his church or any other. Preparing for that day's message, with a feeling of utter inadequacy, he was driven back to the words of Christ Himself. He read them over in the final minutes of solitude before the service. A low bustle of voices began, as people filed into the pews. The organist played a solemn prelude by Saint-Saens.

Throughout the service, his attention kept drifting to pockets of empty seats among the congregation. It was undeniable evidence that things were not as they should be—in spite of the easy rationalizations to which he was prone (that the younger couples could not afford homes in the area, that "numbers" were not important, and that the city's population had diminished because of the recession).

When it came his time to speak, he felt vulnerable, as if half the congregation might be staring intently at his balding head. *What would happen*, he wondered, *if someone should mount the pulpit and begin to rant and shout, in the manner of some of the black ministers he occasionally heard on AM radio, and whose ability to emote and to move people he admired.* This, he had always known, was not and could never be his style. Rev. Wharton looked into the familiar faces of people who sat in the same seats each Sunday, ever since he could remember. They seemed one person, one face.

"Matthew six, thirty-three," he read, in the King James Version he still preferred for public oratory. "Seek ye first the kingdom of God, and his righteousness; and all things will be added unto you."

He allowed a long pause to let the words sink in before continuing. A few people squirmed.

"This passage is well known to us—perhaps, to the point of obscurity. By 'all things,' the Lord was clearly referring to the necessities of life. But do we—and I want to emphasize that I include myself—do we really believe that this is the Christian position? If any of you hearing this today say *yes*, then you have taken a truly radical stance."

Shaking hands on the church steps, it struck him that everyone said the same things: *enjoyed your message*; *thank you for that word*; *very timely*; and so on, after any of his sermons. On many days, he would have preferred an outright argument—one of Greg Stuart's barbs even—to the same old bromides.

The stack of mail waiting on his desk the next day depressed him—more. The title *Reverend* was a magnet that attracted junk mail by tons: clever schemes to boost your church's income; slick brochures advertising baptistries; "Dear Pastor" letters from scores of organizations, all in desperate need of money by three o'clock that afternoon. He separated the wheat from the chaff, leaving a large brown envelope—obviously something different—to the last.

PRAY FOR THE NORTHWEST CRUSADE said the poster. He shuffled through the other material from the Billy Graham Crusade office with ambivalent feelings. He had never been a fan of great, huge gatherings, and disliked the adjective *mass* when applied to things spiritual. But he left the material on his desk, and before he left for visitation in the hospital that day, he affixed the Graham poster to the church's bulletin board.

One evening toward the end of the week, after he had given the matter further thought, Keith Wharton drove his car into the Stuarts' drivew: / unannounced—Elton being one of the few people he could talk to freely.

"Nonsense, Keith," Elton told him when he began unloading his feelings. "You are a good preacher—and a fine teacher as well. You've opened up the Bible for all of us."

"Thank you for those kind words, Elton, but I have recently realized that ministers are just about the last Santa Claus image left in this world. What people don't know, though, is that behind the mask, this clergyman," he pointed at himself, "gets headaches like everybody else, sometimes has X-rated dreams, and on most days, feels decidedly . . . what shall I say? . . un-Christlike."

Elton, out of uniform and in casual clothes and slippers, had pulled himself out of a comfortable reclining position while the minister spoke.

"Why are you telling me all this?"

"Because confession is good for the soul, as they say. And," he placed a hand on Elton's shoulder, "because I trust you, my friend."

The minister took a few steps and stood near the arched opening of the fireplace, directly opposite Elton. "And it will give you some basis for understanding the request I want to make of you."

Elton's head had tilted to one side, and slightly back. A log in the fireplace popped, distracting Wharton for an instant. "I would like to see our church choose to participate in the Northwest Crusade."

It took several long seconds before Elton could answer. "You expect Billy Graham to revive you?"

"Now, Elton, look. I realize that evangelism has never been my immediate thrust. I'm not looking for some panacea, but I think it's evident that . . ."

Elton interrupted. "That whole atmosphere . . . I don't know, Keith. It just goes against the grain. It's so . . . well, it's so *unlike* us." When the minister did not immediately answer, he added, "Don't you think so?"

"I think you can be as ineffective on a one-to-one basis as you are in a crowd of thousands if you are not spiritually motivated. Elton, I know this constitutes something different for us, but I'm not telling you all this on a whim. I've considered it all very carefully. I need you to help me bring the people along."

The fire was almost out. A single lick of flame threw shadows across Elton's face, making it difficult for the minister to register how his friend received it all.

"Will you help me, Elton?"

9

The television might as well have been in his room. The commercial for designer jeans came on for the third time. Scott fixed his eyes on the ancient typewriter, but the sultry words swept his mind away. *Professional advertisers*, he thought, *certainly knew how to turn heads.* The apartments quieted down for a while, then the whimsical musical prelude to a "M*A*S*H" rerun broke his train of thought. It was a program he had always enjoyed. He forced himself to write, the typewriter keys lifting and striking like little hammers.

The Church and Poverty: An Historical Survey

By Scott Stuart
for Dr. Kuhl, Ethics

The record of the Christian Church in dealing with the poor is not one that should elicit any sense of satisfaction or pride on the part of those of us dealing with this problem today. We must, I think, begin with a close look at the root causes of poverty, as found in the Scriptures, and how we have dealt with these causes.

The carriage-return bell emitted a faint *ting* at the end of each line. For some reason, the telecast of "M*A*S*H" died out. He had replaced the washers in the kitchen faucet, and no paralyzing drip hindered his concentration. Gulping a cup of instant coffee and following his outline, he finally got rolling on the essay, bashing out little machine-gun volleys on the battered typewriter, stopping only to untangle the keys. He finished the Introduction, extracted the page, and read what he had done.

The noisy step on the stairs, the apartment's only burglar alarm, gave a distinct creak. Whoever was coming up did so at emergency velocity. Someone rapped at his door.

He opened the door. It was Laura, out of breath, pale and frightened.

"Easy, calm down."

Her explanation of what had happened was a jumble of half-finished sentences. Tugging at his arm, she insisted he come with her immediately. They ran across the street, through a red light, causing a car to squeal its brakes, arriving at her apartment building, huffing for air. The hallways smelled like rotten cabbage.

Mr. Thornhill, an elderly man in the apartment next to Laura's, had stumbled on his crutches, gashing his head open on the sharp corner of a table. Claiming an aversion to the sight of blood, Laura gave way to Scott, who wound an improvised bandage around Mr. Thornhill's head, and managed to stop the bleeding. Scott carefully wiped the red rivulets from his face. He was a shriveled old man, well over seventy, with skin almost transparent and tufts of hair sprouting from moles on his face. Scott thought the old fellow handled it all rather stoically.

"That's got it stopped, Mr. Thornhill, but we ought to take you down to the clinic. I'll get my car and . . ."

"No clinic!" the old man said, eyes blazing.

"You really should go," offered Laura, as if compensating for her squeamishness.

"No way! No clinic. They've been trying to get me out of here for months. They happen to see I'm gone, they'll lock me out."

"What do you mean, 'lock you out'? Who'll lock you out?"

"The ..." The old man's eyes fell on Laura, "the swine that owns this place, or one of his stooges. He keeps jacking up the rent. Since his last increase, I'm short each month."

"They can't just throw you out like that. There are laws, ordinances. Now, look, you need to go to the clinic."

Mr. Thornhill shook his head, his protruding lower jaw locked firm. "No way. No clinic."

Scott looked around the place. It was almost a cell: single bed, hollowed and sagging like a hammock; tiny kitchen with only the bare minimum of appliances and belongings. The stuffy air reeked of stale grease and dirty laundry; dead flies piled up inside the light fixtures. On the dresser, the only piece of furniture in the place not worthy of the dump, stood a collection of faded photographs: a handsome man in a military uniform; a smiling woman, her face framed by tumbling curls; and, in the middle, the two of them holding a baby. Mr. Thornhill noticed Scott looking at it.

"This is what you get for years of service," he said bitterly, forgetting the presence of Laura and adding an obscenity. She did not appear shocked. "Vietnam, Korea ... what was all that? Me, I was in the big one in forty-two! These guys, what do they know? Oh, yes, we were heroes then, believe you me."

"You're sure you'll be all right?" Scott was afraid the gash would start bleeding again.

"Oh, yes, we were heroes then," he repeated before answering the question. "All right? Be all right? Of course, I will. This old soldier will survive. That swine tries to throw me out of here, I'll wrap this crutch around his neck."

Laura told him, "Mr. Thornhill, just bang on the wall if

you need anything."

In a quicksilver change of mood, the old man looked at the two young people, managing a smile. "You are good people. You make a nice couple. Thank you for patching me up. Kind of reminds me of one time back in thirty-eight when I was trying to . . ."

They listened to his rambling story for ten minutes. Scott thought it obvious that he rarely spoke to anyone. They assured him they would see to it that he did not get thrown or locked out.

"Feisty old guy," Scott told Laura in the hallway.

"Really."

A baby cried in one of the flats. In the background, a television announcer bleated banalities, sounding like a sheep through the walls. A man in a suit who looked like a rather angry used-car salesman threatened a cowering woman in a doorway.

"Now you pay or you get out, you understand? *Comprendes?*"

She said something back in Spanish, but he talked over her.

"You tell your garlic-breath husband, or whoever lives in here, that he better steal you some more money!"

She closed the door. The baby's crying ceased. Scott, who had stopped to take in the whole scene, thought it unreal. The landlord seemed out of a cartoon, like the sinister moustached character in cape and top hat who tied widows to railway tracks when they couldn't pay their mortgage. He had never imagined anything of the sort happening in a day of rent control, city ordinances, and other ostensibly humane practices.

"That's real nice," Scott said almost involuntarily. "Attacking people at night. You do this all the time?"

"I have to do it when the food stamps and welfare offices are closed. What's it to you?" His thick eyebrows bunched together. He gave Scott a little shove in the chest. Scott waited to see if he would knock on Mr. Thornhill's door, but he lit a cigarette and stomped off, casting the two of them a look of undisguised hostility.

"Nice guy," said Scott when he was out of range.

"Very."

On the way downstairs, he got a laugh out of her by saying that it was obvious the landlord had not composed the words to "All You Need Is Love" or "Where Have All the Flowers Gone?"

"You hungry?" he asked.

"Yes." Her color had returned. She looked almost cheerful, hopelessly out of place in the dismal surroundings. Another baby started to cry. Voices seeped through the walls.

"Then come for dinner, at my fabulous penthouse."

She took his hand. They stopped and bought barbecued chicken in a take-out place that had an old Otis Redding song blaring inside. "IT'S THE WATER!" said the blinking neon beer sign out front, which Scott read aloud for no apparent reason. She thought this somehow brilliantly witty. He found it easy to make her laugh.

"Your steps creak," she said.

"Steps? The whole apartment creaks."

She helped him clear peanut butter jars, dirty dishes, and other debris off the table. They lit a candle, dining in a pool of light.

"Better this way. Can't see the rest of the place."

"I like your posters."

"They're functional. They cover holes."

"Oh? I like that one. I'd like to go up in the Space Needle sometime."

"Why don't we?"

"Really? Why don't we? Yes, let's do it."

Scott polished off a drumstick and started on a wing, washing it down with a soda. The plastic mug boasted a Seattle Supersonics emblem. "How did your folks ever let you move down here?" He looked at her wide, ample mouth; her teeth were perfect.

"They don't know I'm here. They think I'm tucked away

in a nice little condo. Actually I was. I rented it to three University types for seven hundred a month."

"You're kidding?"

She shook her head. "I'm making money. At least they'd admire my business acumen. But if Daddy knew where I lived he'd probably . . ."

"Hire a S.W.A.T. team to follow you around?"

"Right," she laughed. "You know, he might be right, too."

"Why do you do it?"

She took her time answering, "I wanted to find out if I could manage, you know, down here. I really needed to know—for me—what my commitment was to Christ. Or maybe if I even had one. I don't know. Everything had always been so easy."

Scott sat back and crossed his arms, listening.

"But I wonder some times, to tell you the truth. I have this recurring dream . . ."

"You don't by any chance mean the feeling that all you're doing here is some kind of self-righteous posturing?"

"You, too?" she said.

"Me, too. But you know, I really don't feel like talking about it right now."

"I don't either."

He moved toward her. She sat passively at first, then followed his initiative. They kissed, accompanied by the noise of cats fighting on the roof.

Long after Laura left that evening, Scott's term paper was still unfinished. He couldn't seem to concentrate on anything or anyone but her.

10

Agnes Speilman, a spry lady in her fifties, wearing blue velveteen shorts, eyed a high-bouncing return. She scooted around to her good side, and struck a firm, clean shot that Greg purposely let go by.

"You see?" he told her, pointing with his racket. "It makes a difference when you take that shot on your forehand, doesn't it? You should do it every time you can, till we get your backhand in just as good shape."

"You absolutely bring out the best in me, Greg. I'm ecstatic."

"You might need a lawyer pretty soon. You're going to start beating your husband."

"Oh, Greg!" She gave a high-pitched laugh, donning a sun visor and dark glasses. "Thursday at five?"

"Thursday at five."

Agnes was one of the better students of the game, a quick learner. With others, it was all he could do to maintain his composure, or, alternately, to keep himself from bursting out in laughter when they struck home-run balls over the fence or ran the court with all the grace of a baby hippo. *Better, though,* he thought, *to teach menopausal ladies than share a hold with a cargo of stinking salmon.* He headed for the locker room and a long-awaited shower. Sheila intercepted him.

She wore a pair of tight designer jeans. Greg imagined her emerging at the end of a line of cosmeticians, coiffeurs, and fashion specialists. Nothing was out of place. He wondered how old she was. He guessed in her late twenties. She was so perfectly "turned out," it was hard to tell. Shifting his eyes, he noticed she wore a new ring. Her words flowed smoothly, confidently.

"I think Mrs. Speilman would like to have you for dinner."

He had not known she had been watching. "Yeah—she really makes those old bones move."

"Are you going to clock out now?"

Clock out. Greg thought it sounded a bit odd. "Yes. That was my last appointment."

"Why don't you come over to the house and join me for a drink?" She phrased the question like a statement, as if the outcome were a foregone conclusion. "Sort of wrap up the day," she added.

"Sounds like a winner . . . how do I get there?"

"Meet me on the pier in fifteen minutes, okay?"

SERGIO VALENTE. Greg read the label over her gently swaying rear pocket, as she walked off, her thick mane of dark hair bouncing. He watched her until she passed out of sight.

He quickly showered and changed. The Ivygate Club had its own docking facilities on Lake Washington. He waited for her there, feeling a bit silly. She pulled up in an open power boat.

"Where we going? Hawaii?"

"No time. Our place is on Mercer Island."

She drove flat out, giving other craft a wide berth, leaping swells, crashing down into others, sending up sheets of spray in the late afternoon sun. White caps scurried across the lake. The two of them conversed in abbreviated yells over the noise. Behind and above, on the Lacey V. Murrow Bridge, cars raced on from nowhere to nowhere. Being on the water gave a feeling of immunity from the urban bustle on all sides. Sheila pulled in at a private dock facing Seward Park across the lake.

The Holt-Browning house exceeded his expectations; stately and big, with Tudor-style architecture. There seemed to be acres of rolling lawns, dotted here and there with formal gardens. Greg turned his attention to the mansion. *How much,* he wondered, *did it cost to bring all these building materials out here?* The entire layout gave a San Simeon effect: grandiose, overwhelming, and *very* costly.

Inside, he caught himself staring at the handsome furniture and signed original paintings by famous artists. *This place could be a museum,* he decided. Even a young man from Capitol Hill had to be impressed. The huge house seemed empty of people, not even a servant. He sat down in one of the wingback chairs that flanked the stone fireplace, gazing at a nineteenth century hunt print on the wall. *Country English,* he guessed. *Probably the whole place had been done by a professional decorator.*

"I'm going to make up a banana daquiri," she said. "Would you like one?"

"Got any Bud?"

She looked puzzled at first, then amused at his request. "I think I might. Let me look."

She departed to the bar, pausing to turn on some soft jazz.

"Here you go." She handed him the beer and a wooden coaster with the Ivygate logo. "You don't drink the local brews?"

"Can't stand any of them," he told her. Sheila curled up in a corner of the couch, feet tucked underneath her. Tennis and gossip magazines covered half the coffee table. Greg skimmed the titles, one above a glossy photo of a dimpled television star.

EXCLUSIVE!—MAGNUM'S SURPRISING SECRET!

Another read:

BORG—THE END OF THE LINE?

The jazz played like Muzak.

"How come I never see you out whacking the ball?"

"Oh, I have to force myself to get out there."

"But you do play?"

"Oh, yes," she said, hesitating, as if the question might have been a *double entendre*. She sipped the daquiri that Greg thought looked a bit sickening—an alcoholic accident. "Father managed to ruin my taste for the game. Of course, I never exactly told him that."

"Why?"

Greg's eyes flashed down to the table again.

CONNORS CONQUERS

"Well, I grew up on tennis. Force-fed you might say. By the time I was twelve, I showed some promise, but I think what Daddy wanted was some tennis junkie, you know—a world-beating automaton. I really think he had this sort of hallucination of me curtseying to the Queen at Wimbledon."

Greg laughed and set down his beer.

"Revenge for not having a boy," she said, in a more subdued tone. "By the time I was fifteen, it was pretty apparent that I was not going to be the champion he wanted. All the Holt-Brownings are realists when they crash into a brick wall."

"Oh, I bet you're better than some of those Amazons that show up at tournaments."

"What's the matter," she said, a trace of challenge in her

voice. "Aren't you attracted to competitive women?"

"Well, as long as you can tell they are women without performing a complete physical." He told a few off-color tennis jokes, which seem to amuse her.

"What are you doing for dinner?" she asked abruptly.

He looked slightly stunned. "Well, nothing, I guess."

"Why don't you let me take you out?"

"Why not? Sure, let's go out." He drained the beer.

It was getting dark. A bank of dark clouds spread just over the horizon, a bruise on the sky. Lights from buildings undulated on the surface, like long, glowing water snakes.

"I like the mixture of natural and artificial light," she told him, navigating slower this time, pointing things out.

'So, you photograph things other than jocks playing tennis?"

She nodded. "I find it very relaxing."

Greg was about to add, "You must spend a lot of time in dark rooms," but thought it wise to not risk anything at that point.

"Be ready when I get there, okay?" she said, when they parted at the dock. An Ivygate employee took care of the boat. Greg had trouble starting the motorcycle, and began to think about replacing it. He drove home and changed into his best clothing. Elton was still at the office. His mother fussed over him, brushing his clothing free of lint. He waited, nervous.

SHEILA

said the license plate of the bright-red Porsche. She offered him the keys.

"You can drive."

Incredulous, Greg stared at the car for a minute. He had never been inside such a machine, much less driven one. He tooled delicately through traffic. The Porsche's powerful engine made a noise between a whine and a growl, and responded deftly to steering, brake, and throttle. It made his bike seem something that any mechanically inclined youth might have thrown together out of spare parts and tubing. At Greg's request, she snapped in a Rolling Stones cassette. Greg noticed people looking at him, enviously, and he loved every minute of it.

"Where are we going?"

"Fouth and Leonora."

L'AUBERGE DE LA BASTILLE

Restaurant Français

The place, Greg thought, *merited the term* class. A string quartet played chamber music on a small stage. Sheila looked comfortable, within her natural habitat.

"I like it here," she said in a voice full of money. A waiter, who appeared to know her, guided the couple to a table.

"*Quelque chose à boire ce soir? Ou vin, comme d'habitude?*" he asked.

Sheila thought a minute then replied casually, "*Merci, Gaston. On a du Courvoisier?*"

Sheila asked Greg what he preferred. He said it didn't matter. She changed her mind. "*Champagne, s'il vous plaît. De la maison.*"

Greg scanned the menu, intimidated.

L'AUBERGE DE LA BASTILLE
CUISINE FRANÇAISE ET CONTINENTALE
Guillaume Devanthery, gerente, vous salue

Spécialités—Pâté de fois gras, avec sauce à l'orange. Bifteck le Parisien à la mode, avec haricots jaunes ou escargots.

"Where are the prices?"

She answered with a look.

"I don't see any chili," Greg complained.

"No chili." She smiled.

Gaston brought the champagne. Greg took a sip, noting the whiteness of Sheila's skin. She described the various dishes. He followed her suggestions.

"You know, I've been talking to my father. I don't think he has any idea at all how really good you are."

"Well,' he said, flattered but believing, "you'll convince him. I'm sure."

"What I need to do," she said, sounding businesslike, "is to get you a match with some built-in PR. Then I can nudge Daddy."

Greg finished off his glass, feeling a welcome glow, the sense of being out of his element rapidly abating.

"Until you beat a ranked player, you can't be on the computer."

Greg complained about the computer ranking system, calling it a "video game," and about the bureaucrats in the various tennis organizations. Sheila listened patiently.

"I understand all that, but serious players can't move up without the computer. That's simply the way it is. Oh, you've finished your champagne." She summoned the waiter. "*Gaston, encore du champagne, s'il vous plaît.*"

"J'arrive, Mademoiselle," he said, filling the glasses, leaving the bottle at Sheila's request.

"This," said Greg, pointing at his dish with a knife, "is fantastic. Let's come here again." He downed more champagne.

"I thought you might want to. Maybe we can."

Sheila seemed to maintain a sort of business attitude that Greg found unsettling. He tried to keep her off the subject of tennis and finally succeeded, discovering that she liked to talk about herself. He probed her tastes in music and movies, on which she was knowledgeable and interesting. These themes exhausted, he switched to questions of a more personal nature. She talked about her time at Stanford, the various adventures there. The time passed slowly. Pushing the conversation along, Greg asked her if it wasn't inconvenient, living on the island. Sheila burst out laughing.

"Did you really think I shared living quarters—no matter how large and comfortable—with my *father*? Of course, I do entertain there sometimes. It is convenient to the club. No, my dear boy, I have a town-house." She went on to describe her apartment in a fashionable area of town: its careful decor; the transluscent furniture with the latest in fashion-designer fabrics. She mentioned her modern art collection—one of the finest in the country, she added, not at all apparently trying to impress him.

"Is there anything that you don't do well?" he asked, looking into her eyes, twin pools with onyx islands.

"Not that I don't want to do," she replied, lips parted slightly, as if reading underlying meaning. Her eyes narrowed. The business inflection in her voice had vanished.

"How are you at contact sports?" she asked.

11

"**I**s something wrong with Keith, Elton? He didn't seem himself."

He told her about the Crusade, how Keith wanted him and the entire church involved. She seemed less than enthused with the idea.

"It all seems so very important to him," he said.

"I suppose it will be men on one side of the room and women on the other?"

"With name tags," he added.

"And they'll probably be singing all those jingly, infantile choruses."

"Anne, I really don't know that much about it. I do know that it is important to Keith. Sometimes we forget that he has concerns and struggles the same way we do."

Anne started to say something, but Elton had turned the other way, unintentionally cutting her off.

"I think," he said, "I'll look in on our resident athlete."

At the mention of Greg, Anne seemed to drop her complaints. She continued reading James Clavell's *Noble House*. Elton paced to Greg's room, wincing at the loud music that emerged. Greg turned it down and set aside a racket with which he had been tinkering. He was pleased to see his father, something that Elton found gratifying.

"I know it's late. I just wanted to say, 'Good night, Coach.'"

"Oh, Dad. Can we talk a minute?"

Elton marveled at the way working at the club had smoothed some of Greg's rough edges.

"Sure, son. What's on your mind?"

"Well, every morning when I pull into the club on my bike, this parking attendant gets this smirk around his pimples. I guess what I mean to say is, I really need a car. Now, I know I had the loan at graduation, and I'm still into you for the ski equipment." He stopped a moment. "I wouldn't need a big sedan or anything."

Elton let the request hang in the air before replying, "I'll ring Ray Cooley in Purchasing. If there's a company car available, we might get a good break there."

"Anything to keep me out of the wind."

"Well, we can always inquire. Good night, son."

Elton started to close the door.

"You know," Greg said, "they really think I'm good over there."

Elton shrugged. "They do? Amazing. I could have told them that right from the beginning." Greg was startled at this comment. He had always thought he never did *anything* right in his father's eyes.

Elton left early the next morning to beat the traffic. He pulled into the lot of the high-rise office building that housed Minute Man Life.

RESERVED—E. STUART

In the lobby he bought a coffee and a *Wall Street Journal*, which he began to read in the elevator. In the solitude of his office, he perused the stock prices, then read an article on Paul Volker of the Federal Reserve Board. A busy day lay ahead. Madge, his secretary of many years, informed him that he had a number of calls on the recorder. *Easterners,* Elton thought, *they never knew what time it was on the West Cost.* More than once he had been startled awake by some impatient and incredulous executive in Boston or New York, oblivious of the rotation of the earth, and the breadth of the United States.

"Madge, have Ray Cooley call me, will you?"

Finishing his coffee, Elton swiveled his chair around, enjoying the panorama of the city he had lived in all his life. The broad shoulders of Mount Rainer in the distance stood out, in spite of a wisp of smog, a detail that depressed him. It had not always been so. He had seen the city change radically in his lifetime, but the air was clean enough for him to pick out the stars and stripes flapping proudly in the center of the Kingdome roof, beams extending from it like spokes of a wheel. Farther to the south lay Boeing Field. His view purposely excluded the Space Needle, which he thought too modernistic, an exaggerated frisbee on a tripod. The new Rainier Bank Building he likewise thought inferior, with its strange pedestal that gave it an upside-down look. He preferred older architecture, such as the Smith Tower, built in 1914. Turning his attention to the desk, his eyes caught a group picture of the family, prominently displayed. It was the last photograph of them together.

Elton began mentally composing a directive to the sales force concerning group health insurance, a policy Minute Man Life planned to drop. The subject had been a source of argument with Scott, who favored government insurance, a position contrary to Elton's political and social views. Elton knew Scott would see Minute Man Life's abandonment as a proof text. Ray Cooley called and said he had a few spare minutes. Elton dictated his memo as he walked through the outer office, now abuzz with activity. His presence had the effect of making people speed up, or stop talking,

"Are you ready, Madge?"

"Yes," she said, pen poised above a steno pad.

"To the sales force: This is to advise you of a corporate policy. Effective as of the first of the year, we will no longer be involved in group health insurance. I trust that the sales force will honor this decision and shift their attention to areas more profitable to themselves and the company. The usual signature."

In the lower concourse of the building, Ray Cooley, clipboard in hand, led Elton along a row of company cars, stopping at a four-door Chevy. Elton kicked a tire, and gave the vehicle a quick inspection.

"The interior looks fine but what's under that hood? You wouldn't sell me a ringer now, would you?"

Cooley gave an easy laugh. He was a frisky man in his midfifties, efficient, congenial. "No. Sam O'Brien's meticulous. Not on the road too much. Doesn't smoke either."

"Well, I'll mention it to Greg. How have you been doing anyway?"

In the course of the conversation, Cooley mentioned that he was working on the Graham Crusade. Elton pressed him for more information as to how he had become involved. Cooley stopped walking and turned toward him, speaking earnestly.

"In 1950, when Graham was thirty-two years old, he was in Portland on one of his Crusades. They had to put up this temporary building because no place in town could handle the crowds. My father pounded nails for them, and I came along to see what all the fuss was about. Jesus became real to me during those meetings. Yes, it was the summer of 1950 ..." Cooley started to say more, but realized he was holding Elton up with his enthusiastic memories.

"Listen to me carry on," Ray said. "I better let the executive go back to his job."

"Oh, no, Ray. Not at all. I'm glad you told me all that, I really am."

Elton finally made up his mind on the way home. He

waited until after dinner to tell Anne. Sensing her reservations, he stressed his desire to help Keith.

"You know, I wish they'd think of another name for those things other than *crusade*. To me, it smacks of the Middle Ages or these far-out nuts. I can just see it, people pouring in here from everywhere, making jokes about the rain we've heard a thousand times but they think are so funny."

"I don't know if there's any call to be so strident about it," he said.

"I just . . ."

"Don't you think you might be overstating your case?"

"I'm not overstating my case, Elton. I'm trying to *state* my case."

"Well, it's clear you are troubled."

"Elton, I am troubled. Would you like to know why?"

"Yes, of course. Why?"

She hesitated, as if the answer were so completely obvious, he might say it himself, but he maintained his inquiring expression.

"Elton," she said, looking him full in the face, "where are you going to get any more nights?"

12

Anne's normal shopping technique was to know what she wanted, get it, and retreat home. She disliked the way some of the younger women became denizens of malls, seemingly born to shop. Contrary to her custom, she drove to Pioneer Square and walked around, looking in windows, wasting time. Little she saw merited her attention or money. She and Elton had almost everything anyone could sanely want, and the other things—giant-screen televisions, video games, pens with digital watches in them, and other faddish gadgets, seemed frivolous.

She stopped under an old Victorian iron lattice work, where people used to wait for streetcars on the cobblestone pavement. The arched grills above divided the view into squares, like an atlas map. She considered having coffee at a corner cafe, but changed her mind and continued plying the stores, letting her mind wander. The sky which had been crowded earlier was now fully closed. It began to rain, not really falling, just "there." A sign on her left read: BOOKS.

She went in.

The magazine stand gave her a kind of mental indigestion. *How could people read all that trash?* she wondered, surveying the names of the publications with their glossy photos: *Hot VW's, US, Latest Song Hits,* and *Rolling Stone,* the latter with a photo of a popular punk musician, earring through his nose, and wearing an expression of such fathomless stupidity that it almost elicited feelings of pity. She picked up an exercise book.

SIX WEEKS TO A BEAUTIFUL FIGURE!
In this issue—JANE FONDA TALKS
ABOUT HER NEW EXERCISE BOOK.
ALSO—CYCLAMATES IN FOOD—NEW CONCERNS

They always featured an anatomically perfect woman on the cover. Anne thought it a reverse form of pornography and left the stand, looking for some serious fiction. She bypassed the spin-offs of last year's best-sellers. A book display near the checkout caught her attention. She examined the novel.

In Glass Houses is the first book of a genuine artist. Riley Wyndham shows insight and maturity rare among today's writers.—*Los Angeles Times*

People have not heard of Riley Wyndham, but they will.
—*Denver Post*

A Lewis and Clark journey into the modern soul. *In Glass Houses* is well worth reading.—*Toledo Blade*

Opening the cover, she began the jacket review.

"Excuse me, anything I might help you find?" a man asked.

"No, thank you." She looked up briefly, then back to the book, her memory registering a face. Head oscillating, she compared the black and white photograph on the dust jacket with the clerk standing in front of her.

"Excuse me, is this your book?"

"Yes," he beamed, "I hope it's not my last."

Anne emitted an involuntary gasp. She had never met an author before. He was tall, angular, with a sort of refined, rumpled appearance, the way she imagined authors should be. His thin hair had begun a retreat back across his head, but this did not detract, but rather, she considered, *enhanced*, the lean face. The corduroy jacket and sweater were the same, she felt sure, as in the photo. His English accent, distinct but not exaggerated, pleased her ear, used to Elton's American corporatese.

"You . . . work here as well as write?"

The author looked momentarily uncomfortable. "I'm afraid so. You see, with literacy on the way out, most writers need some sort of outside sustenance to survive. For now, I'm no exception, but there is cause for optimism."

"This synopsis certainly seems interesting. And I like your title."

"It's not doing too badly at the moment. So far—knock wood—some favorable reviews. One critic called it a kind of Lewis and Clark expedition through the modern soul."

"Very impressive."

"I try to deal," he said, appearing to scale down his words, "with the way people can break out in their own way."

Anne thought this a bit general, but said, "Who could resist that? Of course I'll take a copy."

At the register he asked her, "Have you heard about our literature seminar?"

"No, I haven't. Please tell me about it."

He handed her a bulletin.

"We meet here, once a week, just a few local people and the odd literati. I give a short talk, then we discuss books, authors, our feelings, anything, but mainly literature."

"I was a literature major. Of course, that was some time ago."

"I think you'd find it quite stimulating . . . May I autograph your copy?"

"Oh, yes, please do."

"Your name?"

"Anne, Anne Stuart."

"That's a good Scottish name."

Riley signed the book in neat, flowing letters. He appeared eager to talk further, but a squat woman summoned him to the classics counter. He left begrudgingly, saying good-bye to Anne.

Anne walked through the rain to her car, the book in hand, the notice of the seminar tucked into the pages. She sensed an emotion vaguely familiar—but long absent. Someone had left an advertising flyer under her windshield. She removed the soggy thing and discarded it.

At home, she set aside *Noble House* for *In Glass Houses.* Elton arrived late. Anne realized she had neglected dinner and hurriedly threw some meatloaf into the oven. Throughout dinner, Elton was uncharacteristically grumpy and laconic. He flopped out in his favorite chair afterwards, drifting off to sleep to a recording of Mahler's Ninth Symphony. Anne heard him get up later and go to bed, but kept on with her reading.

Riley's style was spare and taut; his characters were well drawn and carried the plot well. Knowing the author, more than anything else, kept her forging ahead, enthralled, chapter after chapter. She did not see Elton's silhouette in the doorway.

"Anne?"

He startled her.

"Yes?"

"Anne, are you coming to bed?"

She looked at the clock. It was 1:45 in the morning.

13

It rained the night before the match. The day dawned with a sky the color of steel wool, but the curtain of clouds parted by mid-morning. A patchwork of sails covered Lake Washington. A procession of luxury automobiles began to file into the Ivygate Tennis Club.

Since Sheila had arranged an opponent, Greg had cut back on his lessons to train and practice. Mornings found him jogging miles through Madison Park. At the club, he logged hours on the ball machines and lifted weights. Fredericks appointed himself coach, something that annoyed Greg at first until the manager showed him an error in his backhand on videotape. Greg, setting aside his adversary mentality, allowed Fredericks to work out with him, practicing those shots that gave him trouble. The rigorous training, however, left him sated with the sport. He saw himself in dreams, his mouth opening and a racket emerging. In another bizarre vision, he sat in the *Auberge de la Bastille* with Sheila. Everyone wore tuxedos and evening gowns, but he

93

sat there in shorts and a shirt with an alligator over the pocket, head ringed with a necklace of orange tennis balls. Gaston, the waiter, brought a platter covered with smelly sweat socks. They all began to laugh at him, so hard that the walls of the place shook. Sheila tried not to laugh, like someone stifling a sneeze, but soon howled with the rest of them. With such nightmares disturbing his sleep, Greg followed Frederick's advice that he not overtrain. As the contest drew close, he played just enough to keep a fine edge on his game. Sheila nagged him to get enough rest.

His opponent, with the prosaic name of Ken Smith, was the reigning gladiator of another prestigious club. He had won enough to place him among the proletariat of the computer-ranked players. Greg had never heard of him.

The stands were packed to capacity. Temporary seats had been installed at court level. Photographers set up their gear behind the baseline, and at the net. Professionally sanctioned officials would oversee the play. Greg sought refuge from the throng in a corner of the locker room.

He tried to pre-play the match in his mind, visualizing important shots. His foot twitched up and down involuntarily. Every few minutes Fredericks poked his head in to tell him how much time remained, like a stage manager readying the lead actor. The locker-room door opened.

"Ten minutes, Greg."

He was tired of sitting. His palms had started to sweat. He went through his final stretching exercises and stepped outside, where Sheila awaited him in the corridor, camera in hand.

"Don't go out there yet. I want the other guy on the court first. Let him be the one to get impatient. I want the crowd to work for you."

"How many of his 'fans' are here?"

"Don't worry about it. I've seen him play. I know you can beat him."

Fredericks, lurching nervously, came around the corner.

"Five minutes, Greg. The other guy's on the court.

They're waiting for you out there."

Sheila squeezed Greg's biceps, as if infusing him with additional power. Setting down her camera, she threw her arms around his neck, breathing in his ear, "Blow him off the court for me." She left. Greg hesitated a moment, took a breath, then stepped out in full view of the crowd.

Agnes Speilman and her cheering section composed of Greg's regular students clapped wildly, faces radiating sheer adoration. Mrs. Harrison, one of the wealthier ladies, stood to reveal a red T-shirt, which she had monogrammed:

GREG!

Greg acknowledged the applause. Sheila took her place up high, with the VIPs. Her father, Roger Holt-Browning, sat regally erect, arms folded, taking in the proceedings. He held something in his hand that Greg thought might be binoculars.

"Go, Greg!" the ladies chorused.

"Silence. Silence in the stands, please. Mr. Stuart will serve to start the match."

Greg took the early lead, piling up service aces. Smith proved a strong hitter, but lacked mobility. Greg won the first set rather easily at 6-4, but sensed a change in the momentum toward the end, when Smith seemed to gain confidence and settle down.

In the second set, Greg suspected that someone had been secretly supplying Smith with scouting reports. He kept hitting to Greg's deep backhand, still his weakest stroke in spite of Fredericks' coaching. Smith baited him into numerous unforced errors; he grew frustrated. During a break, Fredericks suggested coming to the net more often, insisting that he had the speed to get back, should Smith try to lob over him. Greg agreed, and followed the strategy.

Then Smith also began coming to the net. The match became a slugfest at close range—two heavyweights rocking each other with blows. The ball barely touched the court on some points. Greg had his serve broken, but immediately broke back. Smith disputed a call on one ace, arms out-stretched, voice whining. The umpire put him in his place, threatening a penalty point. Greg stayed at the baseline and tried to keep his opponent moving, coming in only when certain of making an easy volley into the open court. But Smith showed patience and experience, outlasting him to take the second set by a grueling 7-5 score.

In the early going of the third and final set, Smith's fans became more vocal, inspiring their man. Very quickly, Greg fell behind 3-1, angry at himself for needless errors, telling himself to settle down. Bouncing the ball before his serve, wiping the sweat out of his eyes, Greg felt a resurgence of strength. His supporters made their own comeback. Agnes looked as if poised to leap onto the court and turn a cart-wheel, like an undergraduate cheerleader in the NCAA tour-nament. They hollered and screamed like roller-derby fans, doubtless partly from sipping cocktails through the first two sets.

Knowing Smith could not be relied on to beat himself, Greg took the game by the throat, attacking Smith's passing shots as if they were an evil force to be destroyed. When a simple touch volley would suffice for a point, he whipped powerful overheads that caromed up into the stands. The crowd loved it. Cameras clattered like empty machine guns. Greg battled his way toward match point. He looked up. Sheila held clenched hands to the sides of her face, bouncing up and down in her chair. Smith was not about to con-cede, but he had lost concentration. He threw up desperation lobs that Greg whacked for easy winners.

"Double match point."

They chanted for him.

"Silence, please."

Greg drove a shot that barely ticked the sideline. Smith again resorted to a lob. Greg faked a smash, let the ball bounce, then two-handed a bullet that handcuffed the star-tled Smith, and punctuated the match. The cheers swal-

"Mom asked me to find you. She wants us home for dad's birthday."

"Man, I'm not the present he wants."

"Since it seems that we're possibly going to see you only once every few months...well, it concerns us what you're going to do with your life at this juncture."

"Dad, you've worried about me for twenty-one years. I'm relieving you of the responsibility. Why does it always have to be questions and decisions? Can't you just back off?"

"I was in the city today...had lunch with Daddy. You know, I don't think he realizes yet how really good you are. What I need to do is arrange a match for you..."

> "What does this place have to offer to someone of your potential?"

"I want to be
down here for
these people. I
want to live it
out...all of it."

"Why do you get
so bent out of
shape every time
anybody talks
straight about the
Lord? I've got it
figured out, man.
Your quarrel's not
with Jesus. It's *dad*
you can't stomach.
It's authority that's
got you all balled
up—you've got the
two all tied
together."

"Does the Ivygate club know that its hot-shot pro is an up-and-coming wino? I don't know, son. You have a real talent for upsetting me."

"I don't know, dad. If you want to be upset about my being an adult, I mean…there's not much I can do about that, is there, now…"

"You can acknowledge twenty years of every possible advantage... privileges that were both costly and paid for. You can acknowledge your Christian background, and the fact that your family deserves more from you than just booze and dope!"

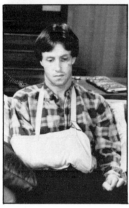

"You know, I... I...have...been attempting to destroy myself... I'm not sure why..."

"If there's one thing I would like you to remember from this night on, it's this: that whatever you've done... whatever you've thought... God loves you. Whatever your condition... whoever you are... whatever feelings you have in your heart right now... God loves you."

"Some of you have been playing it the world's way for years. You've tried it all—and you've come up empty. Let Jesus Christ fill all those empty places tonight."

"I'll tell you one thing—I can't make any sense out of any of this... without you."

lowed up his yell of pent-up emotion. He tossed his racket high among the spectators.

"Nice game," said Smith, when they shook hands at the net.

Everyone poured onto the court. A mob of admirers followed him into the clubhouse where voices babbled, glasses tinkled, and imported champagne flowed in rivers. Sheila worked her way through the jubilant entourage, took Greg by the arm and ushered him over to her father, a tall, distinguished-looking man, graying around the temples, and wearing an English blazer with a stylized crest on the front.

"Daddy," she said, beaming, "I'd like you to meet Greg Stuart."

His handshake was firm. "Congratulations. A strong game always whets my appetite. I must say, your strategy out there was most impressive."

"Thank you, sir."

"I understand my daughter is your representative. We'll be meeting again, I'm sure."

"I'll look forward to it, sir."

A photographer pushed through to take shots of the trio. Sheila drew Greg away from the others and kissed him violently.

"I knew you could do it."

He quipped. "Did I do it out there or what?"

"I saw it all. You did it even better than I thought. You did have me worried in that second set, though."

"I was never in doubt."

"Listen," she said, looking around, "some of Daddy's USTA buddies are here. Some real biggies. I think I better circulate." She lowered her voice. "We'll celebrate later—alone."

"There's someone I want to tell. My brother."

"So call him. Tell him you'll be on tomorrow's sports page."

"I want to see the look on his face. He lives down in Factorytown."

The word punctured her ebullient mood, like a hair on a dinner plate. "Look, I don't want to have to sweep you up some place." She handed him the keys to the Porsche. "We're partners now. Go tell him on four wheels. But try to keep it under a hundred, okay?"

"No problem."

She lightly nipped his earlobe.

"I'll be waiting for you," she said. "Don't be all night," she purred invitingly.

"Don't worry. I won't." Greg was torn between longing and driving that car.

He strode into the lot and stopped beside the Porsche, admiring. There wasn't a speck of dust on it. It's red finish glistened. He got in and revved it up, watching the tachometer needle jump, feeling the throb of the exhaust and the smoothness of the seats. He snapped in a cassette of *Jumpin' Jack Flash* and let it blare. At first he cruised slowly, nose slightly elevated, enjoying the way others turned their heads to look. Then he increased his speed, weaving in and out of traffic joyously. He continually switched lanes, much to the annoyance of other drivers. Crossing the bridge to Factorytown at seventy miles an hour, he finally slowed down, reluctantly, as he neared Scott's. Parking in the rough part of town, he locked both doors. He eased around a puddle in front of the apartment. Scott ran out in response to his honk.

"I did it!" he yelled, running out.

"Did what?"

"I beat a ranked professional!"

Scott bounded down, whooping.

"I blew him off the court."

"I don't doubt it." Scott eyed the Porsche. "What is this? The prize?"

"Jump in. I'll tell you all about it."

"I've got to be at the University in forty-five minutes."

"Well, *come on*! I'll have you there in ten!"

"Bring me back?"

"Of course."

Greg put the Porsche through its paces, gunning hard over the University Bridge, until the engine screamed. Scott hung on to his seat.

"Man, this thing's like a little jet plane."

"Moves doesn't it? It's one of Sheila's toys."

"The hyphenated photographer?"

Greg nodded. "It is not good for man to live alone, saith the good book."

"Are you one of her toys?"

"What is that supposed to mean?"

"You know—kind of a live-in leisure accessory?"

"Scott," he responded, looking straight ahead, "let's face it. We can't all be Mother Teresa in pants."

They pulled in to the University. Scott checked his watch. "New world record. Let's go."

"Who'd you say was lecturing?"

"Billy Graham. I was assigned to come." He held up a pad. "I'll be taking notes."

Greg slowed, and looked momentarily disoriented, like a teetotaler who suddenly found himself in the midst of a rousing Oktoberfest. "The big Graham cracker himself, huh? I thought it might be a debate, godless humanists versus Jehovah's boys."

They were among the first there. They sat talking quietly, digressing from details of Greg's match to Thoreau's religious beliefs to recent popular films. Students, a few media people, and scattered faculty filed in, filling the place. Graham sat for part of his lecture, appearing relaxed and at ease, drawing some laughs with a remark that he had vowed to make no jokes about the rain during his stay on the coast. He listed his main points on a blackboard, telling the audience that he had himself gone through a period of doubt about Christianity and the Bible, especially over Christ's claim to be the Truth and the only Way to God. Greg listened to the explanation of faith and nudged his brother.

"Isn't this the usual line? I thought you weren't interested in 'mainstream' Christianity."

"Can we just *listen* to the man?" he answered, able only with difficulty to keep his voice a whisper. A woman two rows down turned and frowned at them.

Graham cut his lecture short and opened it up for questions. Hands shot up and some people spoke out loud, like journalists at a presidential press conference. The evangelist signaled a girl in the front row.

"Mr. Graham, what is your view of the resurgence of the religious right in this country?"

Graham cleared his throat and said, "Through the years many people have asked me to crusade against various evils. My plan is to go to the heart of the matter, not just deal with the symptoms."

"But you are not yourself a member of the Moral Majority?"

"No, I am not."

An irate student with a thick foreign accent took Graham to task for his recent trip to the Soviet Union. The youth, turning a bright red, like a lobster, and getting more unintelligible as he spoke, enumerated the evils suffered by believers in the entire eastern block. Graham let him have his say, adjusting his glasses as he listened. A rumble of impatience passed through the lecture hall. People looked at each other and shook their heads.

"The guy talked for five minutes," Scott said.

"Now, what was the question?" said Graham to some scattered laughter, quickly turning serious. The audience appeared to be on his side. "Let me say that I am aware of everything you mentioned and more. There is by no means the same amount of religious freedom in the Soviet Union as in the United States, but neither are we perfect. I could give many examples but I suspect all of you here are well aware of them. I knew the potential for misunderstanding of the trip was there, but I felt it was worth it to preach the Gospel of Jesus Christ to people who have had less opportunity to hear it than we in America. Next question, please."

Graham handled a series of queries on subjects from television evangelists to the disarmament debate, all the way to his opinion of the current pope. No one heckled or became abusive. Greg shocked his brother by putting up his hand. Scott tried to become invisible by shrinking down in his seat.

"Yes, this young man over here," the evangelist said.

"Mr. Graham, are you aware of the account of the death of Henry David Thoreau, when someone asked him if he had made peace with God, and he replied that he was not aware that they had ever quarreled?"

Heads turned toward Greg; a number of people laughed.

"Yes, I read it when I was a student. Now that was a few years back . . ."

Greg interrupted. Scott hoped he wouldn't say something outrageous.

"Yes, but what is your view of the myriads of people like Thoreau who are theists—purveyors of truth—and yet not subscribers to your style of religion?"

The evangelist smiled and spoke to Greg as if he might be the only one in the room.

"What about them? They all die. There is a common denominator for all mankind—the moment of our death. It happened to Thoreau. It will happen to you—me—to all of us in this room! 'There is a time to be born and a time to die.' The ultimate test of our truth will come when we face God. And the choices we have made in this life will have to stand for us, or perhaps fail us, in that supreme moment when we meet our Creator!"

Others continued to raise their hands. Greg said that he should be getting back, but Scott held him off long enough to hear the response to a question about the fairness of the Reagan budget. He scribbled notes that looked like Arabic characters.

"Why didn't you bring a recorder?"

"I left it in the car, and somebody stole it."

"You wanted to live in Factorytown." They left the lecture hall and headed toward the car, feeling the tension between them.

Greg broke the awkward silence in the car by turning on

the radio. Scott lowered the volume. They started debating issues, and by the time they got back to the apartment, it had grown into an argument. Greg's glib style turned back Scott's accusations that he was scared to face God, and that he "got bent out of shape" every time someone tried to talk to him about Jesus—something Greg vociferously denied, contradicting himself with volume.

"You don't define who you are," said Scott, taking a different tack, "by things—or how successful you are—or how good you are at sex. That feeds your ego. It doesn't add up to your soul."

"Will you get off your high horse? What are you? The Vice Squad? You know, Thoreau wrote about 'reformers' like you. Said they were bores. I don't have your tolerance for boredom."

"Life's a lot of things right now—but *boredom*—not even in my vocabulary. I'm opening up doors for myself, Greg, and Jesus moves in—and He lets me know that He is there. The love—you can almost touch it. What do you think He's going to take away?"

"Look, stop the lecture, okay?"

Scott got out of the car, shut his door, and walked around to Greg's side. "I've got it figured out, man," he said, lapsing from the approach he had employed to that point by raising his voice. "Your quarrel's not with Jesus or God—it's with Dad. It's authority, isn't it? You've got the two all tied together."

"Fantastic." Greg nodded cynically. "That's deep, Scott, really deep. Profound, in fact. Write a paper on it. Now, if you'll excuse me, I have to go. Don't want to keep anyone waiting. I've got some serious celebrating to do, and you've got your paper to write. Later."

Disgusted, Scott threw his notes on the sidewalk angrily.

Greg spun his tires going out of Factorytown. Crossing the bridge, he began to fantasize Sheila awaiting him, appropriately attired—and alone. The vision filling his mind, he tooled swiftly through traffic, sure of his destination.

14

A nne made dinner reservations at Rosellini's Other Place, planning a midweek surprise for Elton, who had been behaving rather morosely of late. She thought an evening out would be good for him. This done, she took a long luxurious bath in the spacious antique tub with the curved legs and faucet that filled in the middle, not the end. Emerging, she toweled off.

Whenever Elton seemed distant, she tended to suspect herself, that she was gradually becoming less attractive to him and everyone else. Still, exercises and jogging had kept her trim. Her face was remarkably free from lines, flesh still taut under the chin. Anne scented herself and selected a black, strapless dress from her wardrobe. Fully prepared, she relaxed with herbal tea, reading a short story by Jorge Luis Borges in *The Atlantic*. The telephone rang.

"Darling," said Elton on the other end, a sure harbinger of bad news. "I've been looking over my schedule. This week is going to be absolutely chaotic. I'm going to be late in town

Tuesday and Thursday, possibly even on ... Anne, are you there?"

"What do you want me to say?" she said after a long pause, before hanging up. She stood there a minute, arms crossed, then flung a pillow across the room in disgust. She called the restaurant, canceling the reservation, then sulked in a chair.

For a moment, she entertained the thought that Elton might have an amorous relationship with another woman. There were, she knew, enough of them around, although the closest, Madge, his secretary, certainly posed no threat— unless, possibly, Elton's eyesight had grown bad. She wondered if that situation might be easier to deal with than having Elton married to a corporation and subject to its slightest whim. Another woman would be a recognizable foe, whereas a company was an impersonal, vague entity, with many and varied powers. Dwelling on it made her angry; she forced herself to think on other matters.

The folder she had used as a marker stuck out of her copy of Riley Wyndham's novel. She opened and read it. The literature seminar at the bookstore was that evening. If she hurried, she would not be too late. She deliberated a moment, but recalling Elton's phone conversation, she put on her coat and drove off. The automatic garage door closed behind her.

Anne felt slightly frightened walking alone through Pioneer Square. Two drunks on a bench sang a ribald song. A policeman approached them. The bookstore appeared closed and dark inside but the door was open. She went in. The lights were dim. Candles burned on tiny tables. About twenty people were there, mostly women, thirty-five and older. The scene seemed strange to her; a combination classroom, bistro, and bookshop. Riley Wyndham paced back and forth giving his talk, hands in his pockets, a red scarf around his neck.

"Oh, I fully agree with that statement. *Being There* is a delightful, brilliant book. But the thing that is so very remarkable about Koszinsky's writing is that English is not his native language."

Anne's entrance halted him.

"Ah, we have a visitor. Welcome! Please have a seat."

He smiled at her a second, then swung back to his talk. "Since this is such a rare gift, do any other polyglot authors come to mind?"

A woman with glasses thick as the bottoms of Coke bottles asked who had written *Lord Jim* then answered her own question. "Joseph Conrad. Another Pole."

"Yes, indeed. In his case, English was his *third* language after Polish, of course, and French. Quite a feat, really. Makes you wonder where all the Polish jokes come from, doesn't it?"

Anne laughed with the others. She had known that Conrad was a trilinguist. Riley changed themes.

"Now, Conrad was a nineteenth-century writer. What about this whole question of modernity in literature? Some people take the rather puritanical view that everything written now is trash, while other critics contend that we are in a kind of 'Golden Age.' Any opinions on this?"

He turned in Anne's direction. "Anne Stuart," he said, cutting off the woman with the thick glasses. What might your view be?"

They all turned, awaiting her comment. She felt uncomfortable, almost as if on trial, and it was a few seconds before she could bring herself to answer.

"Well," she said, organizing her thoughts, "I really think that sort of thing has to be left to posterity. I think survival is a big test for any work of literature."

Riley appeared impressed, and interjected, "That is a good point. Yes, this Golden Age concept could be nothing more than an advertising gimmick, in the final analysis."

The group, Anne noted, hung on Riley's every word. They laughed at his advertising line. Anne sensed an insurgent freedom of expression and continued without inhibition.

"Look at C. S. Lewis, for example. Everything he wrote:

well, *almost* everything, is still in print and selling well. My son even used *The Discarded Image* as one of his texts in college. Can any of us imagine our grandchildren doing postgraduate work on something like *Valley of the Dolls?*"

Riley laughed and clapped his hands together, delighted at her answer.

"That's not to say," Anne went on, now feeling completely at ease, "that there is no quality work being done. I just finished a work titled *In Glass Houses* that I think will be around for a while."

Wyndham basked in the applause that followed Anne's statement. "I'm sorry," he said, holding up his hands, "any further outbursts of this nature and I shall be forced to cancel the entire series."

A gaunt woman with a constellation of moles on her face asked what C. S. Lewis had written. Wyndham momentarily looked like a teacher about to send a student out of the room. He pointed out a shelf of Lewis's works, made some remarks about the subject of the next lecture, then brought the meeting to a close. Disengaging himself from the woman with the thick glasses, he made his way over to Anne.

"So good to see you here, Anne. And thank you for those kind words. That is very heady praise indeed. You'll never know how writers appreciate such things."

"I liked it very much. I want to read it again."

"Will you come to our next meeting?"

"I may be busy that night, but I'll certainly try."

A short, paunchy man, smoking a pipe with a funny bend in the stem, drew Riley to one side. Anne mingled with the others, who all urged her to return.

"I loved your line about *Valley of the Dolls*," said a friendly woman in a white turtle-neck sweater. "It really is *ghastly* rubbish. I can't imagine anyone reading it not sitting under a hair dryer."

Anne agreed with her.

"I'm writing a book," she continued, "about a woman who is obsessed with that sort of thing. She reads drugstore novels, then proceeds to live them out in her own life. I'd really like it to be a statement about art, and how it relates to current life-styles and neuroses."

"That sounds interesting."

Anne looked at her watch. She waved good-bye to Riley, then slipped away before the opportunity arose for someone to persuade her otherwise. The anticipation of what Elton might say robbed her enjoyment of the evening, but when she arrived home, the house was still empty. She quickly changed clothes and turned on the television to a documentary about panda bears in the Chinese mountains. Elton arrived just after nine.

She balanced the desire to tell him where she'd gone against his offenses of working late and neglecting her. She felt a strange combination of guilt, frustration, and a need to be close to her husband—the latter feeling eventually prevailing. When Elton appeared to fend off her overtures she told him where she had been earlier in the evening, surprised at his nonchalant reaction. She took the issue no further. Elton read the latest issue of *U. S. News & World Report*, then went to bed, falling fast asleep. Anne lay awake beside him. When she had barely drifted off, a loud *thud* awoke her.

"Elton," she whispered. "I think I heard something."

He grunted and rolled over. A stumbling noise came from the foot of the stairs. Elton finally responded to her prods, got out of bed, and walked to the top of the staircase. Anne sat up, listening.

Elton discerned Greg wobbling his way up.

"Greg? What's the trouble?"

He did not answer. He looked disheveled, as if he might have been frisked by three people at once.

"Greg, are you all right? You look as though you might have had a pretty rough night."

"Hi, Dad," he slurred. "How ya doin', old Elton John? You want to update my file, too?"

Elton put his hands on his hips. "Your mother and I were asleep. Now what have you been drinking?"

Greg stopped, leaned against the banister, appearing to be in deep thought, as if actually trying to recall the name of some exotic beverage. His father loomed large at the top of the stairs.

"Or smoking," Elton contemptuously added.

"You forgot 'snorting' and 'shooting' didn't you? Let's be thorough now, okay? Cover all the options."

Greg moved up a few steps under Elton's hostile gaze.

"By any chance, does the Ivygate Tennis Club know that its hot-shot tennis pro is an up-and-coming *wino*?"

"Oh, that's *good*, Dad. That's a real zinger. Who writes your material, Dad?"

Elton's lower lip curled. He italicized every word. "I don't know Greg. You have a real talent for upsetting people."

Greg moved past him with some difficulty. "I don't know, Dad," he said, imitating the preface to Elton's last statement. "If you want to be upset about me being an adult, then there's not much I can do about it, is there?"

"Not much you can do about it?" Elton said, barely restraining himself from yelling. "You can start by acknowledging twenty-one years of every possible advantage! Privileges that were both costly and paid for. You can acknowledge your Christian background, and the fact that your family deserves more from you than what we might expect from any slobbering stumblebum on Skid Row—booze and dope!"

Greg lofted a finger in Elton's face and shouted back. "Look, this family has only produced one real Christian. And it is not *you*!"

They stared at each other, neither backing off. "What you've got," Greg snarled, "is more on the ornamental side, with a little tinge of hypocrisy."

Elton drew back his hand and cuffed him across the face. Greg tripped backward and fell down. He held his face and glared at Elton for a moment; then got up and strode past him into his room, leaving his father standing there, staring off at nothing. Elton rejoined Anne, who sat up, rigid and nervous, having heard it all.

Elton, weary and angry, crawled back into bed. Both he and Anne were too wrought up to go back to sleep, though both pretended to. After lying stiffly on his side of the bed for a while, Elton turned to her and said, "I wonder if it's true?" losing his anger and becoming suddenly analytical, staring up at the ceiling. "You know, an interesting statistic crossed my desk the other day. Minute Man estimates that the cost of replacing a burnt-out executive ranges between two hundred and fifty to five hundred thousand dollars." He looked briefly at Anne, then back up at the ceiling again. "I was just wondering how much I'm still worth."

Anne rolled over to hug him. He finally fell asleep, but Anne not at all, the incident with Greg provoking a swarm of fears.

Elton, in spite of his difficult night, went to work early the next day. Anne knocked on Greg's door, telling him it was almost nine. She heard no response, and thinking that her son slept off the previous night's adventures, left him alone. She returned a few minutes later, knocked, and hearing nothing, opened the door.

The room appeared to have been looted. Greg had gathered his things and slipped away. He had scrawled a message on the mirror.

SORRY MOM

She stared at the letters incredulously, unable to hold back tears. She felt herself in the throes of a dozen different emotions, alternately accusing herself of being selfish for wanting Greg home at all, to blaming Elton for driving him away. She faulted the way they had raised him, thinking that if they had done a proper job, Greg would have little interest in wild living. Wiping the words off the mirror, she began to cry freely, then left the room as she had found it.

She sat looking out the window, trying to think, and to pray, reading a selection from a devotional:

*O God, when my heart is faint, and I am overwhelmed,
lead me to the mighty towering rock of safety, for You
are my refuge.*

She turned the phrases over in her mind, but the house
seemed to echo with last night's arguments, and to teem
with the ghosts of past quarrels. The Queen Anne chairs and
other antiques seemed props for some tawdry, plotless
drama. She had to get out.

Seeking a diversion, she drove downtown and walked
aimlessly, looking in windows and at people. Occasionally
there would be a face that would seem to understand her, a
moment's eye contact, recognition, then gone forever.
Drunks bore their expressions of bottomless woe. She noticed that some of them were quite young, whereas they had
once all seemed so old. Pigeons swarmed for crumbs, the
colors on their necks flashing. Observing the women shopping in their chic designer jeans and Gucci boots, she at-
tributed to them a trouble-free life of blissful consumption. A
sign proclaimed:

FOR THE WOMAN WHO HAS EVERYTHING

"Anne!" came a voice from behind her. She turned
around.

Riley loped up, his face crinkled in a wide smile. He wore
a rust-colored jacket, a green sweater, and tan corduroy
slacks. His presence startled her at first. She had been intro-
spective to the point where she lost track of location.

"Anne, it's so good to see you. You look so very charm-
ing today. I was just slipping out for lunch. Would you care to
join me?"

"Thank you, Riley, but I was really just passing by shopping."

"Oh, please," he pleaded, "I'm in need of some good, in-
telligent conversation. All morning I've been deluged by
obese, obnoxious women! You must come with me."

She reflected a moment. His smile was infectious.

"Well, why not?"

They walked to a nearby cafe, sitting by a window where the bright rays of the noonday sun warmed them. They found themselves talking about television programs, the vast majority of which they both despised.

"It's amazing how blindly anglophile Americans can be. They think everything from Britain is good, but of course it is not. 'Mahstahpiece Theatah is made possible by a grahnt from Mowbill Corporation.' They assume that whatever follows that is the very zenith of artistry."

"How are things going? Financially, I mean."

"Much, much better, thank you. The other day I even turned down a review. First time I've ever done anything like that."

"Can you afford to be choosy now?"

"Not really, but you know as well as I, that it is futile to waste criticism on unrelenting imbecility. I told the editor that if he wanted to call this feminist tract 'literature' that was fine with me, but I preferred to refer to it more accurately as 'clerical work.' "

Anne laughed. "You should have taken it and written something completely scurrilous—maybe that you suspected that the book had originally been written in crayon, or something along those lines."

Riley swallowed his tea and laughed loudly, going into a minor coughing fit. "*Written in crayon*," he said when he recovered. "May I have your permission to use the line sometime?"

"I hereby grant you all rights and privileges. I'm not a writer, just a reader."

"You're more literate than some writers and teachers I know, and that would include some of my former colleagues at the city college."

"Oh, don't exaggerate. I don't read everything. I don't have a favorite contemporary Russian novelist."

"Just as well," he said. "I doubt if you'd find their 'girl

meets tractor' themes of much interest. I certainly don't."

He told her of plans for a sequel to *In Glass Houses*, and the possibility of persuading his publisher into making it a trilogy. She listened, fascinated, enjoying the breadth of his imagination, daring to make suggestions, which he appeared to take seriously.

"We should go, Riley. They are very busy."

A row of patrons waited for seats, anxious to gulp something before returning to the office. One woman loudly complained that someone had been seated before her, and that she had arrived first. A man at the next table picked his teeth.

Riley edged his hand toward Anne's. She saw the move and reacted by opening her purse.

"Here. I'll leave the tip."

Riley paid the bill.

"You've no idea how you've lifted my day," he told her outside.

"And you mine," she said.

"Will I see you at the next meeting?"

15

"**M**y dad's always hated the thing."

Scott stood with Laura on Queen Anne Hill, viewing the skyline to the Southeast, dominated by the Space Needle. They had dedicated the entire day to prowling about the city, a break from the burden of studies.

"I don't know," Laura said, "I kind of like it, really. It certainly is different." She took a photograph with an old Canon.

"I don't know anything about cameras," Scott said, handling it, pointing to the various dials. "How does it work? Is this one hot and the other cold?"

She laughed and explained its mysteries. "Here, take my picture. It's all set. You just focus and shoot."

"You sound like Cheryl Tiegs doing a camera commercial on television."

"Too bad I don't look like her, too."

"Oh, I don't know. I think you are all right the way you are."

Scott framed her in the viewfinder. She stood like a

statue. "Oh, come *on*! Give me some emotion!" She attempted to strike a pose. Scott affected an accent such as he thought a fashion photographer might have. "Geev me *l'amour*, geev me daring. That ees eet! More! More! Geev me animal magnetism, *ma cherie*."

Laura's laugh turned into an adolescent half-giggle, half-squeal. She bent over, weak of knee and rib. Scott tripped the shutter. She demanded that he pose. He seized a bottle in a paper bag, a discard of some alcoholic, messed up his hair and slurred his speech as she readied the camera.

"Low-life Beer from Filler. The best thing about it is—it makes you drunk!"

"Stop it!" She was unable to hold the camera steady.

"Everything you've always wanted in a beer—and worse!"

Laura controlled herself long enough to take the shot. They joined arms and walked along.

"Anybody ever tell you you're crazy?" she asked.

"I only act this way when I'm under a heavy load. My mind feels like a hothouse. Everything coming in, nothing going out."

"I know what you mean."

They stopped at the park's contemporary sculpture and read the plaque.

Changing Forms

Sculpture by Doris Chase

It looked like a gigantic cube, drilled through from all directions, topped by a short length of dowel that had also been perforated.

"Now this I definitely don't like."

"Well," Scott said, trying to be objective. "It's not bad if you look at the skyline through it."

"I don't think that is what Doris Chase had in mind."

"Probably not. Come on, I'll show you another viewpoint."

The lawns glistened with little beads of water. Jets soared aloft from Boeing Field. As they walked, Scott discoursed on the history of Seattle.

"What's that down there?"

"That's Gas Works Park. Capitol Hill is back farther that way."

"I'm really starting to like this city," she said. "I think I could live here."

"Really? Where do you want to go now?"

"I don't know. You are the guide. Lead on."

"Want to see the houseboats at Portage Bay?"

"Not really. Why don't we go up in the Space Needle?"

"You *are* a tourist, aren't you? Why don't we throw the frisbee for a while. I feel like running around."

"Yes, why don't we, while it's not raining."

They flung the projectile back and forth. Laura slipped on the wet grass, staining her crisp new jeans bought with the proceeds of her subleased condo. Scott's tosses kept coming back to him like a boomerang. Every time he tried to balance the spinning disk on his index finger, he failed. Laura, far more athletic, showed a variety of curving throws, and dexterous catches behind her back.

"Look," she said, pointing at a passing automobile, "a group of Christians."

"What? Did they have one of those little fish on the back?"

"No, they had a dog and a station wagon. That puts them in the Kingdom doesn't it?" She shed her light jacket. Her hair nicely framed her face. With her soiled knee, she reminded Scott of the neighborhood girls he played with in his youth.

"I can see why you picked a school away from your Calvinist father. I thought *I* was bad."

They drove to Seattle Center. Laura asked Scott if anyone ever called him "SS" for short. He told her the preference was "Scotty," with numerous friends requesting. "Beam me up, Scotty." She laughed at his Star Trek imitations. They played a game of changing around the beginning consonants of names. Dolly Parton became Polly Darton; Johnny Carson, Cohnny Jarson, and so on. Scott, with identical consonants, claimed immunity, but Laura concocted Stott Scuart. She then became Jaura Laffe. It was great fun. They pulled into the Center's crowded parking lot.

"Ever climb up there?" she asked, high in the observation deck of the Space Needle. Mount Rainier was visible, but wreathed in clouds.

"No. You have to watch it on the glacier. Somebody gets killed every year."

"I want to do it sometime. They just don't have things like that in Illinois."

"What do you climb there? Silos?"

She gave him a playful shove. He feigned fear of dashing himself on the concrete below. Squads of tourists, mostly Japanese, passed through, clicking cameras and looking out with binoculars. Some of them wore Mariners baseball caps. Scott and Laura took the elevator down.

Munching hot dogs, they sat and watched the International Fountain, which sprayed to the accompaniment of music, changing tunes and formats every few minutes. A group of obviously narcoticized youths with "KISS" and "THE WHO" T-shirts ran around under the water with umbrellas.

"How do you communicate the Gospel to people like that?" Scott asked.

"Good question."

The hurtling water and music relaxed them, as if swishing clear their overcrowded minds. The sun was pleasantly warm. They stayed there, discussing some of the points made by Dr. Kuhl, a popular professor, in their Ethics course.

"When I have serious misgivings about this whole Poverty Project, I really appreciate the way he shows historically and from the New Testament that concern for the poor *is* in the mainstream of Christianity."

"I thought we weren't going to talk about that today?" Scott said.

"Fair enough."

They spent the rest of the afternoon touring Pike Place Market and the Seattle Art Museum. A marble ram from the fifteenth century Ming dynasty held vigil over the gates of the latter. Inside, viewing the mostly oriental exhibits, they got into a complicated discussion over whether Francis Schaeffer's theories of art and alienation applied in countries outside of the Judeo-Christian tradition. This theme exhausted, they invented names for books that certain authors might write. Scott suggested she submit her ideas to *The Wittenberg Door*. He let her drive his car home.

Laura insisted on paying for dinner. Scott reluctantly agreed, but stipulated an economical Chinese restaurant. They brought the food to Laura's apartment and watched a special Saturday edition of "Monday Night Football" on her tiny black and white TV. They turned the volume off to avoid Howard Cosell, for whom they shared a common dislike.

"Those New York people think all the rest of us are yokels," Scott said to justify his stance. They listened to the play-by-play account on radio, with often hilarious results during commercials. The screen would show a bottle of beer, while the radio played an ad for synthetic motor oil. They both shook with laughter. During the second half, she sat close to him and popped Fritos into his mouth.

"I had a great time today," she said at the end of the evening.

"Me too."

Halfway home, Scott remembered he wanted to borrow *Psychology as Religion: The Cult of Narcissism*, and lend it to Greg, but thought that he would get it some other time. It would be a good excuse to visit Laura again. The dented Olds that had been swiping his parking place was gone, and he jubilantly pulled in.

Scott had obtained a copy of the city ordinances governing landlords, tenants, and eviction. He studied the documents, discovering that many people were ignorant of their rights under the law. Some had been evicted simply because they could not pay, while the more rapacious landlords

sought to dislodge others in order to sell their units as con-
dos, or, as one developer put it, "affordable housing."

Concerned about ever-speedier evictions, the students
involved in the Poverty Project met during the week and decided to distribute printed copies of the ordinances in their
respective areas. The following Saturday, Scott summoned
Laura early. At breakfast in a McDonalds, they outlined the
areas for the day's work on a street map.

"How about you take this side, and I'll take the other side,
and we meet at the end?" Scott asked. "Or do you want me
to go with you? Maybe it would be better if . . . "

"No, what you said first. We'll cover more territory that
way."

They temporarily parted company.

At the first door, Laura stood rigidly for a moment, sum-
moning the courage to knock. Nobody was home; she gave
an inward sigh of relief and passed on to the next place.

"We're not Jehovah's Witnesses here," a cantankerous,
wild-haired woman told her before she could explain anything. "Get lost," the tenant said, slamming the door.

An unshaven man, still in his undershirt, accepted her offering without comment at an upstairs unit. At the next, a
woman took the paper gladly and thanked her, which boost-
ed Laura's spirits considerably.

She scaled the lower steps of a dingy fourplex. The porch
was covered with old chairs, tires, a disassembled Harley-
Davidson motorcycle, and a pair of rusty car bumpers. The
wooden railing bore a series of black streaks, where cigarettes had been left burning. The name RICK had been carved
with a knife. She knocked.

A dog, very large (judging by its sound) barked twice,
then began a menacing growl. A rough, female voice told the
beast to shut up. The door opened, revealing a man of about
twenty-five. He had a long, thin beard and tired, sagging eyes.
His hair was swept back over his head into a ponytail held in
place by an elastic band. From a leather vest protruded pale,

bony arms tattooed with skulls, eagles, and the name DOTTY. His wallet was bound to his belt by a chrome chain thick enough to hold an anchor. He held a can of local beer and a cigarette in one hand.

"What can I do for you?" he said, revealing a mouth full of rotting teeth. Laura felt a surge of revulsion. She handed him the paper, explaining what it was.

"Is that right? Here, come in for a minute. Honey," he called into the kitchen, "come and take a look at this, will you?"

Laura took two reluctant steps inside. The apartment smelled like an ashtray. A poster of Loni Anderson had been pinned up over the couch, next to a framed picture of a motorcycle. A German Shepherd dog trotted out of the kitchen. Laura froze.

"He won't hurt you."

A woman followed a step behind the dog. She had on tight cut-off denim shorts. One of her eyes had been blackened. A butterfly had been tattooed on her left shoulder. Her rust-colored hair badly needed washing. The dog walked over to Laura, who stood paralyzed.

"Killer!" she said, in a deep, gruff voice. "Get out of here."

She whacked the animal with a rumpled magazine. The man of the house went into a room and turned on the television. "Now, what did you say this is about?"

Laura haltingly repeated herself. The lady asked questions, holding her face disconcertingly near, leering, breathing alcohol and tobacco fumes into Laura's face.

"You thirsty? Want anything to drink or anything?"

"No, thank you. I've got a lot of area still to cover."

"You sure now?"

"Yes. Thanks for your time."

Laura left, went around a corner and leaned against a building, her heart pounding, noticing that she was perspiring, even though it was a cool morning. She pushed the vision of the woman's obscenely smiling face out of her mind and forced herself to go on.

Most people seemed not to care, but took the notice anyway, more often than not shifting their attention immediately
back to the television. This appliance was found, she discovered, in literally every apartment—even if they lacked everything else. The work became drudgery, but the few genuinely
grateful people made the effort rewarding. A pretty, divorced
woman, hearing that Laura was from a seminary, bombard-
ed her with a series of questions about God and the Bible.
She was thoroughly confused, and possessed literature from
a dozen sects and cults. "I just don't know what to believe
anymore," she said. Laura requested a time to come back
and talk to her, and she agreed. A baby wailed in the other
room. She could smell soiled diapers. As she left, two trim
young men wearing white shirts and ties dismounted their
bicycles. Laura looked back; they knocked on the door of the
divorcee's apartment, books in hand.

Toward the end of the morning, Laura flopped on a
bench, exhausted and hungry. She took out a small Testament and read it, waiting for Scott, who was nowhere to be
seen.

Scott had taken more abuse than Laura. He reluctantly
entered another apartment. The paint on the walls was badly
peeled. Aromas of exotic foods filled the hallway. He
knocked on one door; nobody was home. He tried the next
apartment, where the 2 on the door had swung around on its
single screw, so that it looked like a 5.

A crowd of expressionless oriental faces greeted him.

"Uh, English?" he ventured.

The heads shook in unison. Some of them said, "No
English."

"Chinese?" he tried. They all looked blank. The younger
ones smiled up at him. "Well," he said, leaving a notice,
"God bless you."

"Can't you read!" shrieked a crazed-looking man pointing to a sign.

ABSOLUTELY NO PEDDLERS ALLOWED!

Scott left without comment, frustrated and embarrassed. He plodded on, hoping this effort would make a difference in the lives of some of these people.

"Why, thank you," said a woman hanging up clothes. "I didn't know they had to give you that much notice. John, that's my husband—he's in tool and die work—it's been pretty tight lately. God bless you, young man."

That positive response inspired him to go on. Just knowing one person was appreciative was an incentive. At one door, he heard barbershop quartet-style gospel music. A rotund man examined the paper suspiciously, eyes narrowing to slits. He looked only about thirty-five, but a ring of fat bulged above his belt, like excess mortar to be cut off with a trowel.

"Are you associated with any organization or group?"

Scott told him about the seminary, and his church affiliation.

"I see. And you see this sort of thing as part of your ministry?"

"Well, people should have shelter. It's a basic human need."

"Come in for a moment, won't you?"

The place was squeaky clean. A scrawny parakeet squawked in a cage suspended from the ceiling, above a goldfish bowl. The man turned off the music and picked up a Bible, which Scott saw was a *Scofield Reference Edition*, and placed it beside him, as if he might need it.

"Don't you feel," he asked, "that God's order is for conversion first, then social works second?"

"I think some people use that line as an excuse to do nothing," Scott told him. "I've been converted. Now I'm trying to do some so-called social works. I don't want to see people who are vulnerable treated unjustly. All we are doing is informing them of their rights under the law. Is there anything unbiblical about that?"

"No, 'Be subject to every ordinance of man for the Lord's sake,' Peter says. I will say, though, that this sort of thing does tend to be on the liberal side."

Scott waited for him to produce a proof text.

"Would you like to have a word of prayer before you leave?" the man asked.

"Certainly."

Scott listened to the prayer, which he felt might be directed more at him than God. ". . . and help him to do *Thy* will, O God, and *Thy* will only."

"Amen," Scott said, shaking the man's hand and departing.

Passing between buildings, Scott saw Laura waiting for him on the bench. He hurriedly covered the rest of the block and rejoined her.

"I asked this one guy," Scott told her, "what he thought of all the apathy down here."

"What did he say?"

"He said, 'Who cares?' Another guy suggested I might have canine ancestry. 'We're trying to help you,' I told him. He says, 'We don't want to be helped.' He said some other things I won't mention."

Laura took a deep breath, "Let me tell you what happened to me this morning. I . . ."

"Don't tell me. Somebody try to pick you up?"

"Hmmm. Not exactly." She told him about the divorcee interested in the Bible, and the tattooed lady of dubious sexual preference, and about the German Shepherd dog with the endearing name of "Killer."

"Killer, huh?" Scott laughed. "We should go together next time."

"Why?" she said with a little pout, "did some temptress try to lure you inside?"

"Well, you know one *might* have," Scott said jokingly.

Laura looked at him seriously. "What did she say? Some double-entendre?"

"No. She said, 'New in town, sailor?' "

Laura threw back her head and closed her eyes in laughter. She leaned up against Scott and squeezed his hand. "You know," she said. "I really like being with you."

"It's kind of a bizarre date, isn't it?" he said, giving her a little hug.

They left the rest of the notices at a bus stop. When they had turned the corner, a gust of wind scattered them like fallen leaves.

Later that evening Scott worked on the final draft of an important paper. He was just covering a mistake with a blob of white guck when the steps creaked. Footsteps stopped outside his apartment. Someone rapped heavily.

"Who is it?"

"I got some questions about this," a voice said. One of their printed notices slid under the door.

Scott assumed it was some distressed tenant with questions about the ordinances and what to do. He swung the door open, discovering the man whom he and Laura encountered the night old Mr. Thornhill hurt himself.

"Oh," Scott said involuntarily.

The landlord examined Scott, nodding slowly, "Well, I guess that answers my question right away. It was you."

"Is there a problem of some kind?" Scott said, trying to stay calm, sending up a silent prayer.

"A problem? Yes, in fact there is. Now, you have some objection to property owners doing as they please with their own property?"

"No, but some people don't know that they have rights too."

The landlord's eyes seemed to light up. He smelled heavily of some sort of cologne. "What do you care for? Huh?"

"We just . . ."

"What are you? Part gook or something? You sure don't look like a nigger. What do you think you are doing here?"

The light was on in the Robinson apartment. Scott knew the sound carried right through the walls. "Look," he said, raising his voice a notch, "there are laws. Landlords can't just come and . . ."

"Hey!" The man picked up the paper from the floor, crumpled it into a ball and bounced it off Scott's chest.

"You have no idea what we can do," he said, pointing and holding his hand like a pistol. "Now let that paper lay right there." He backed off a few steps. "Kid, I don't think we're gonna be talking again. You just had your only notice."

"Good," Scott said when the man passed out of sight, remembering he had legal rights. He went back inside and sat down at his typewriter, surprised that he was not afraid. Another noise broke the silence. His kitchen faucet had started to drip again.

16

"You're sure nobody will object to this arrangement?"

Sheila looked at Greg as if he might have asked permission to cross the street.

"Greg, you *can't* be serious? I mean, this is the nineteen eighties. If I want you to live here with me—and I do—then that is my business and yours to work out on our own."

He put his belongings away in Sheila's townhouse, relaxing on the couch, still recovering from the previous night.

"Actually, I was going to suggest it today anyway." She sat in his lap, combed his hair with her hands, then held him to her. "You were pretty ripped last night. I'd rather have you here where I can keep an eye on you."

"You were pretty bombed last night too."

"You're not kidding."

"You're absolutely sure it's all right?"

"You know," she said before answering, ruffling his hair again, "you've got a wave back here that I just love." She pressed her forehead and nose against his. "Don't waste any emotional energy worrying about it. You live here now, and that is it. This is your home."

Sheila connected the phone to an automatic answering device. They remained inside all day, the room dark, soft music playing, fire roaring, rain pummeling the roof.

The following Saturday, Greg taught at the club. The students that day were all children and young people. He found it difficult to lie to the parents about the limitless potential and talent that they never failed to see in their progeny, even if they had barely mastered the correct way to grip a racket. *There was something pathetically absurd,* he often thought, *about the most awkward, inept children being furnished with expensive equipment and pushed into a sport where they were sure not to excel.*

The teenagers were usually teachable, but prone to racket-throwing tantrums. Greg disdained such tactics, but sometimes onlooking parents would encourage, "That's it, Garth, get *mad,* throw your racket! That's the way to do it! Get your feelings out." He hated officiating impromptu matches between them, which they took with deadly seriousness, arguing close calls. Many times, he felt himself close to an outburst.

With no tournaments or matches on the horizon, Greg resumed his regular schedule during the week. The men students, especially the older ones, were a mixed bag. They would be receptive and appreciative of his teaching, showing delight at mastering a new stroke and rushing off to whip some old nemesis across town; or, they could be totally blind and stubborn about their mistakes, to the point that Greg restrained telling them to "give it up" only with great difficulty.

Greg knew, without any doubt, that a percentage of the women cared nothing for tennis and simply wanted to be near him. He found them generally repulsive, with some individuals of quite exceptional horror; pallid women, bodies shaped like mudslides, stuffed into undersized, fashionable clothes; elderly women coiffed like twenty-year-olds, with gaudy jewelry and long talon nails like little ovals of blood.

They would babble about soap operas, exercise classes, vacations to Hawaii, and their sons' law and medical practices. When he showed them how to serve, they would snuggle up against him, giggling like adolescents. And if he tried to escape, even a few minutes early, they would check their expensive watches and say, "Oh, but Greg, we still have lots of time."

But Agnes Speilman and a few others were serious students, made good progress, and provided his most enjoyable sessions. Agnes, with her usual worshipful glow, told him one day, "Your parents are the luckiest people in the world to have you for a son."

Away from the club, life with Sheila kept him constantly off balance. She was possessive, and her appetites were large. They often pursued happiness with such abandon that he found it difficult to make it through the next day. She whisked him through exclusive night spots dropping hundreds of dollars in an evening. They always saw the movies and plays she wanted to see. He bought clothing of a type she had suggested, and for which she invariably paid. She expressed unshakable faith in his sports potential, telling him it was all there for him, and that he merely had to go out and get it, never failing to somehow remind him of her own role.

But she was also capable of ignoring him, and could drift into snappy, truculent moods, warding him off, as a babysitter engrossed in a television program might a pestering child. By their third week together, she disappeared regularly on "business dates."

Checking his list one Monday, Greg noticed a new name, Janis Ritchie, booked for his last private appointment of the day. He arrived late, dreading another wrinkled, bifocaled matron with stars in her eyes.

"Excuse me," Greg asked a teenage girl at the end court, "has a lady named Janis Ritchie been here?"

"I'm Janis Ritchie."

He felt a little rush of excitement. She was the slightest bit on the heavy side, but well formed; her high-cut terry cloth shorts exposed tanned thighs, and the white T-shirt she wore was revealing, to say the least. Her frizzy hair, careless smile, and warm, widely spaced eyes made her seem very young. She twirled a racket around in her hands.

"Well," Greg said, stuffing a ball into his front pocket. "Shall we get started?"

He volleyed with her for a while, further assessing her physical assets, as well as the state of her game.

"Let's practice the forehand, okay?"

When he complimented her on a good shot, she uttered little squeaks of delight. They played well over the allotted time.

"You seem really serious about this game," he told her at the end. "You keep taking lessons like this, and people are going to think you are in serious competiton."

She lightly touched his arm. Her smile nicely creased her face.

"Maybe I am?"

He watched her leave, noting her rather tantalizing walk.

"Who is she?" Sheila said with a slight, rough edge on her words when he arrived home. He had not seen her at the club and did not request that she name her sources.

"Janis Ritchie."

Sheila wore the uncomfortable look of someone who is jealous but does not believe in jealousy. Greg welcomed it; he felt in need of some sort of leverage with her. He changed the subject and acted as if the girl were just another student. Sheila made some quick phone calls then stayed with him all evening.

"What sign are you?" Janis asked at the end of the next session.

"Cancer."

"I thought you might be."

"Actually, I'm a Leo."

"A Leo would kid around about his sign."

Greg was neither of the signs. He thought astrology

mindless nonsense, but played along.

"So what lieth in the stars?"

"The possibilities are endless."

She bent over in front of him to pick up a ball. She took her time, and retied a shoe. Greg looked up to see Sheila approaching the court, head held stiffly, almost goose-stepping in her calf-high leather boots. The veins in her throat stood out, and her nostrils seemed to flare slightly as she talked.

"You've got to come with me now, Greg. You have to fill out some important entry forms, so we can get you seeded."

Greg could feel the hostility rising from her. She spoke to Janis through him. "Once you are seeded," she said straightening his collar, "we can take you off these lessons and start training again."

The two women stared at each other for a few tense seconds. The air fairly crackled. Greg said a cursory good-bye to Janis, who appeared stunned by Sheila's intrusion. He managed one backward glance as Sheila escorted him off, seeing Janis sitting glumly on a bench, bouncing a ball. When the new lesson schedule came out, Janis' name was missing. Her slot had been taken by Donna Blackburn, a frail skeleton of a woman who smoked cigarettes on court, swore like a trooper, and swung at every ball with a two-handed haymaker that almost toppled her over.

The match in which Greg was to play was a long way off, but Sheila began to keep Greg on a short leash. She bought a video player and a carton of movie cassettes, partly, he thought, as compensation for her unexplained absences that increased in frequency. She seemed to have an uncanny ability to read him emotionally, and gauge the level of his frustration. She used her favors (or the Porsche), as a reward for good behavior. He found a way to forget some of his grievances, but often sensed an inner uneasiness with the whole arrangement. A remark of Scott's that he might be a "leisure accessory" came back to him with regularity, but he did his best to deny it.

On a Thursday, Greg guided three bovine ladies through

a paralyzing game of doubles. He kept looking at his watch. The hands seemed welded in place, and he rushed off curtly when the time came. Sheila had driven the Porsche that day, forcing him to use the old bike, which ran rough and frequently stalled. As he stretched a tie-down over his gear, a Cadillac El Dorado drove up. Its window dropped down and music boomed out. The driver turned the sound off, stuck his head out and spoke to Greg.

"So I open the papers to see who the Sonics lost to the night before, and I see this picture of some guy named Stuart who wins some fruity tennis match."

Greg took several seconds to register Tony's identity. His first reaction was to laugh, so out of place did the fisherman seem wearing a suit and tie, and driving such a car. While he stumbled over what to say, Tony carried on.

"And I look again and I say to myself, *tennis player?* The last time I saw that tennis player, he was up to his ankles in fish guts. The only net he knows how to use is a fish net."

They shook hands and laughed.

"You did it, man. You finally convinced me you are not working for the IRS. I'll send a telegram to Cap."

"Thanks. I thought you still wondered about me. Speaking of Cap, how is that old cuss doing?"

"Got a dime?" asked Tony.

Greg was puzzled. "Yes, why?"

"Go call somebody who cares."

Greg looked over the car and whistled.

"Nice set of wheels you've got here."

"You like that, huh? I see you're still riding on two. Guess tennis doesn't pay too much, huh? Ha! Ha!"

"I guess it doesn't."

"I'll tell you, man," he said, brushing a hand over the velour seats, "driving this car is some sensual experience."

"So, I guess you haven't been getting out much lately, have you, if you've been getting your kicks from cars?"

Tony did not get the joke. Greg quickly said, "Salmon must be dancing in the nets for you to make payments on this, right?"

"Payments? What's that? Something you eat? I don't make no payments."

He lit a cigarette and blew the smoke out his nose.

"We're talking strictly cash here."

Greg invited Tony on a tour of the grounds. They walked through the parking lot toward a sidewalk that led to the dock. Mrs. Dortmund, one of Greg's students, was wedging herself into a white Mercedes. She was a large, German woman, with a lantern jaw and protruding chin. She smiled at her instructor, flashing teeth like some benevolent barracuda. "Hello, Greg," she said with a pronounced German *r* sound in his name.

"Hello, Mrs. Dortmund."

Tony dug an elbow into him a few paces later. "That's what you get to work with, huh? Whatya doin'? Having a little play for pay on the side? Come on, admit it! That baby's not your style—*is* she?"

He thought of telling him about Sheila, but guessed he would think it all a lie. "Take it easy. It's a living. And it beats busting your back for slave-driving maniacs like Cap. And by the way, they don't all look like that."

"Yoooo-hooo, Greg! See you next time!"

Donna Blackburn (Janis Ritchie's replacement) called to him. Greg waved and forced a smile. Tony placed his hands on his stomach, feigning an attack of nausea.

"They're not, huh?" he laughed and flicked his cigarette off to one side. His hair reminded Greg of the waterfall style of the fifties.

"So you left Cap?"

"Uh-huh. One day he couldn't make payroll. You know what he said? 'I can't pay you today, but if you need some money I'll lend you ten bucks.' They're all the same."

"So what happened? Your Uncle Guiseppe in Milano die and leave you the shoe factory?"

Tony smiled, gave a little snort, then became business-like. "Let's just say I'm now in a growth industry with good

132

bucks in a short time."

"Growth industry. I see we are talking big-time stuff here."

"Right. Growth industry. Say, ten grand a night."

Greg's head swiveled. He saw that Tony was serious.

"Hey, I got his attention. Look, I admit that it's not for the timid, but the risk is low." Tony lit another cigarette. "And there are times when I can use another pair of hands. Like, for example, on the twenty-second, which is why I'm here."

They started walking. Greg looked straight ahead, wild suspicions chasing each other through his mind. He stopped short of asking for details.

"Why me?"

Tony spread his hands and nearly bowed. "You got brains, man. Look, you're no blood relative to anybody on the docks. And you're not gonna upchuck in your lap or run scared on me."

Greg led him back to his motorcycle. Tony looked at it, put his hands on his hips, and shook his head.

"Pal, you got legitimate needs."

"Tony, hey, look. I'm out of all that. Things are looking good. I'm a tennis player now."

Tony leaned close and put his hands on Greg's shoulders. "Oh, I understand." He snapped into a boxing posture and swung some phantom blows. "You work on that backhand now, hear?"

Greg tensed, momentarily unable to speak.

"Think about it." Tony told him. He walked off a few paces. Greg turned to leave. Tony whirled.

"Hey! You!" came his voice again, reminiscent of Cap.

"Remember," he said, a sly, shifty look on his face, "you said you own me one, goomba."

Greg tried to hold his gaze but could not. He felt strangely relieved when Tony drove off.

The bike refused to kick start, and he had to push it. The motor died twice on the way home. He parked it in a corner of the garage, wishing he had followed through on the company car before leaving his parents' home.

Greg selected an album and let the stereo blare. He was hungry, but found little in the refrigerator. He opened the last can of Budweiser, a substance Sheila had been rationing of late, and munched on cheese and crackers. It was his night to use the car, and he debated what to do.

Fredericks, sworn to an oath of secrecy, had procured Janis Ritchie's telephone number from the office. Greg called her. She talked as if the line might be bugged. There were other people in her apartment. Greg said good-bye and hung up, frustrated. He considered going out on the motorcycle and looking up some old friends, or visiting a singles' bar, but it started to rain. Defeated, he flopped out and turned on the television to a roller derby movie, *Kansas City Bomber* with Raquel Welch.

Half an hour later the Porsche rumbled up to the house. He looked outside and saw that she left it under the carport instead of in the garage.

She carried a pair of packages from clothing stores, and rushed about the place.

"Greg," she said, undressing as she walked, "I know I said you could have the Porsche tonight, but I just completely blanked out on this business date I made last week."

"I don't believe this! Can't you cancel it? I was really counting on going out tonight. I need to get out once in a while by myself, too, you know."

"Oh, I know. And I want both of us to retain our freedom, but I'm afraid I can't back out of this one. It just wouldn't look good."

She went into the bathroom. He followed and stood in the doorway, speaking to her image in the mirror, raising his voice another notch.

"Sheila, what is this? House arrest? Let's be fair about this."

"Look," she whirled around. "I don't know what you are so upset about. How many people would gladly change places with you? Why don't you turn that trash off the television and throw one of those new movies on the video player? That's what I bought it for. I really don't have time to discuss anything right now. Now, if you'll excuse me for a minute . . ."

She closed the bathroom door and showered. He thought for a moment of barging in on her, but realized his tenuous position. Swallowing his anger, he returned to the couch and stared listlessly at the screen, where two women fought, swinging roundhouse rights at each other and pulling hair. He considered one of them as Sheila and rooted for the other. Sheila changed into her new clothes in record time and headed toward the door, saying to him, almost as an afterthought:

"Please stay in tonight. No carousing."

She drove off much faster than usual. It seemed to him as if she had not even been there. Frustrated, Greg shut the television off and broke the silence in the house by calling her a series of obscene names at the top of his voice. He fumbled through his wallet, pulled out a matchbook cover with a number scrawled on it, picked up the telephone, and dialed.

"Hello?" purred a female voice.

"Is Tony there?"

17

Anne and Elton ate breakfast, sharing the paper. She laughed at an Art Buchwald piece and read it to him.

"You know," she added, "I really miss 'Donnesbury' but I think Buchwald is just as funny."

"I don't know. I find him a bit on the repetitive side. Do you have the editorials over there?" Elton asked, swallowing his coffee. He looked at his watch. "Oh, never mind. I should get along. It's all gloom anyway."

Anne kissed him and watched him drive off. She took up the paper again and searched the antique section of the classifieds, circling several items. An ad for an original roll-top desk caught her attention. It was something she had always wanted. The address was only a short distance away, in Queen Anne Hill. She brought along the checkbook.

"The replicas just don't quite make the grade, do they?"

A woman with gray eyes and an English accent watched Anne admiring the grandfather clock in the corner of the room, beside an exquisitely varnished sideboard.

"I'm sorry. I was just looking at your clock. It's lovely."

"I'm afraid it's not for sale. I was saying that the replicas of these desks that they manufacture now are unacceptable substitutes."

"Oh, yes. I agree. Do you mind if I open it?"

"Not at all."

Anne gave it a thorough inspection. She knew what to look for. It needed some repairs and a general refinishing, but she wanted it and knew it would be snapped up quickly. They negotiated over the price. Anne thought she had got a good buy. She dropped it off at a refinishing shop, went home, and called Elton to tell him of her find.

"You don't mind if I'm late at the Crusade meeting?" he said, sensing her good mood.

"No, no, You are involved in it. They'll be expecting you to hold up your end. You can't let Keith down, after all."

"Dear, I'm so glad you understand. I think when this is all over we should take a little vacation, or at least go out more."

"Have a good time," she said.

That evening, Anne was among the first to arrive at the bookstore.

It was the last in the series, and she wanted to be there. Everything was informal. They all sipped tea and nibbled desserts. Classical music played, *a fugue*, she thought, *by Manuel de la Falla*. Anne talked with one of the women of more refined tastes in front of a shelf of self-help books. The man with the crooked pipe stem read a review of Riley's novel from an obscure publication. Riley took the floor.

"I like to think that we've gone beyond the shallow analysis of newpaper criticism. I'd like to say that I've enjoyed these sessions immensely. I assure each and every one of you that I am the one who has learned. With banality pressing on all sides and the fathomless inanities of television the only inkling of literacy some people possess, it is gratifying to find a group that appreciates the finer things."

There was enthusiastic applause.

"Now, all creative people need interaction, and perhaps we can do it all again very soon."

Anne felt suddenly lonely amongst the group. She made the rounds, saying good-bye.

"It feels like the last day of school." Anne told a woman who slipped out with her.

"But no diplomas."

Anne agreed, said good-bye, and walked through the square alone, steps echoing. Fog clung in halos around street lamps. Car lights cut swaths through the dark. The air held a chill breath. She heard a clomping of feet coming at a rapid pace. Riley, slightly winded, pulled up beside her. The lights gave a greenish tinge to his skin.

"Anne," he said excitedly, his throat moving like a pump, "I meant to tell you but I forgot. I found my English copy of *Voyage to the End of Night.*"

"Good," she said, defensively. "I'll look forward to reading it."

She kept walking. He matched her strides.

"Would you care to ... swing by my place and pick it up?"

She read the implication of the words, her mind offering a dozen excuses. "Oh, I'd love to but I'm afraid I can't. I really should get going."

He started his answer before she finished hers. "I deliberately finished early, so you wouldn't say it was too late."

The footsteps furnished a kind of meter to his talk. "The book is tremendously liberating, seriously. I'd love you to have it."

Anne fought off the last bit of restraint and turned to him. "Well, all right. Why not? It's still early. Sure, let's go."

Riley brightened noticeably, as if his task of persuasion had been easier than anticipated. He walked Anne to her car, filling in all the silent spaces in their talk.

"Fine, I'll get my car, and you can follow me."

Riley strode off in his awkward gait. She nearly called out to him, but checked herself. She sensed a confusion of emotions sweep over her. Her eyes caught the yellow caution of a traffic signal, and it seemed to bode a warning and blaze up like the sun, blotting everything else out. It changed to red, a solitary, blood-shot cyclops eye, staring at her, searching, knowing all. She passed through a brief moment of lucidity, then, an overwhelming sadness possessed her. Tears welled in her eyes.

Riley pulled up in an old Morgan sports car, top down, in spite of the cool night. She said nothing, still in the throes of a struggle. Riley's weak smile faded from his face.

"I can't," she said finally, with a slight shake of the head. She found it hard to define Riley's expression. He did not speak but nodded kindly, as if he understood and needed no explanation. His smile returned. He waved and drove off, not looking back, his car leaving a trail of exhaust.

The house was cold when Anne got home, so she started up the furnace. The furnace and ductwork seemed unusually noisy, as if a dozen poltergeists struggled to get out and torment her. She sat still, but her mind raced ahead of her, gathering thoughts, images, accusations, that piled high upon her with no relief. She sat quietly, waiting for Elton to come home.

18

All day Elton officiated at high-level meetings. He often felt that vice-presidents were the *de facto* bosses of the company—the real brains of the outfit—with the president serving only as a kind of figurehead. The sessions dragged on; lunch was brought in. Some of the younger executives used terms like "interface," and "principalize," and seemed, for a reason he could not discern, to preface every statement with the word *basically*. A few of the older ones were incombustible bores. Elton tried to move things along, a referee, stepping in when he thought the verbiage was getting too thick, or someone merely talked to hear the sound of his own voice. He was skilled at this, adept at parrying a remark or anticipating a lull in a speech where he could interject, disagree, comment, or change the subject entirely.

"Madge, hold my calls please," he told his secretary, when the marathon was over. He turned on the radio to a station that played soft, "easy listening" music, leaned back in his chair, put his feet on the desk, closed his eyes and slipped into a light, delicious sleep. His phone rang.

"Mr. Stuart, I'm going home now," Madge told him.

He had lost track of time. His body lobbied heavily against getting up. His mind seemed in a mild daze, and he made himself a cup of tea to get the wheels turning again. He began to muse on the untold hours he had spent in his own private corridor of power, issuing directives, authorizing, promoting, hiring, firing, rewording statements. He thought of the countless conferences; the long-distance telephone calls; the thousands of cups of coffee sipped while reading *Barron's* or *The Wall Street Journal*; the lunches with colleagues at favorite restaurants where he left generous tips (and collected the receipts for income-tax purposes). He considered his title; his substantial salary; the esteem he had won from others—all the badges of his success, stacking everything up against what he thought he had wanted out of life. He asked himself, *What do I want out of life?* Whatever it was, it seemed elusive. It remained out of reach and unattained.

His thoughts turned to preparations for the Crusade. His involvement in it was the latest item on the company gossip network, and he had had second thoughts about participation. He had never felt less like attending another meeting and seriously considered skipping out. His body felt heavy and unresponsive. The thought of a quiet evening at home beside the fire held a powerful attraction. He visualized Anne's surprise; picturing her sitting alone, reading, talking on the telephone with a friend; possibly searching the classifieds of the evening paper for another good antique buy; or watching "Masterpiece Theater" on television. Struggling with this, he remembered the promise to Keith Wharton, and how even Anne had reminded him of it that morning. He would have to attend, having given his word. He stopped on the way, ate a quick meal and drained a cup of black coffee.

Elton expected serious discussion to be the first order of business, but while latecomers filed in, everyone sang gospel song choruses. He remembered Anne's dictum against "jingly" music but soon found himself singing along, caught up in the lively spirit. Everyone was friendly, and no one made regional jokes about the rain, or Seattle's usually inept professional sports teams. Keith Wharton, Elton noted, fairly radiated enthusiasm. Cliff Barrows, a leading figure, took the podium and gave a brief history of the Graham Crusade organization and the number of crusades they had held in three decades—well over three hundred.

"What these crusades are really about is people. People who have needs and who look to God for answers. Let me give you some examples."

Barrows quoted from some of the many letters they had received, telling of changed lives and a new outlook. What impressed Elton most of all was the wide cross-section of society they represented: engineers, insurance men, postmen, computer programmers, students—the list was endless. Elton met Barrows just before the workshop sessions started.

"Executive Vice-President for Minute Man Life? You must be a busy man, Elton. Thanks so much for taking the time to help us. God bless you."

Elton shook hands like a politician and squinted at hundreds of name tags. The workshop sessions carried on late into the night. He had been up since very early that morning, and felt a physical and mental numbness. At an unusually long traffic light on the way home, he started to nod off. A truck honked. The light had turned green.

He tried to make as little noise as possible at home, as if he might be stealthily returning home from some nocturnal tryst. It was dark inside. He slipped off his shoes and started toward his favorite chair.

"Elton?"

He snapped to attention. He had been certain Anne would be upstairs and asleep, and he had been taken off guard.

"I'm sorry I'm so late. Believe me, I had no idea at all how much is involved in one of these Crusades—all sorts of workshops and what have you. Must have met a hundred people."

He could barely make out Anne's outline. He waited for her to say something. "It's a bit dark in here, don't you think?"

"Would you sit down, please?"

The inflection of her words puzzled him. Her voice sounded strained. He sat down.

"Elton, you know the literature classes I've been attending?"

He blanked out for a moment while attending to an itch.

"You *do* know that I've been attending them?" she added.

"Yes, I think . . ." He stopped and blew his nose. "Was it any good?"

"Elton, I want you to listen to me."

"I'm listening."

"I have to tell you that tonight I came very close to going home with Riley Wyndham."

The words "going home" garnered his full attention. His eyes widened, then narrowed.

"Going home?"

He stared at her. Anne's gaze had fallen to the floor.

"Riley Wyndham?" Elton asked.

"Yes, the author, the leader of the group. He asked me to come to his house tonight. I guess he just assumed I'd have no qualms about going with him."

Elton watched her as she swallowed with difficulty.

"Did you?"

"No."

She seemed to be trying to pull her emotions together, and gain control over herself.

"But I must tell you, I love being with him. He's interesting, and I like the way I feel when I'm around him. At least we were sharing something."

Twice Elton started to speak. He leaned back in the chair for a moment, rubbing the tips of his fingers together.

"Maybe I don't understand something," he said, his eyes straying. "It doesn't seem to me that you have committed some grievous sin. Are you asking me to forgive you for something that never happened?"

"I'm not *asking* you to do *anything*." Anne had stood up. Her face was contorted, her eyes glassy, and her voice a high-pitched plea. "I'm *telling* you. Elton—if this house is going to be nothing more than some kind of a motel, with the two of us here just ... existing, and not knowing each other, then I don't know if I am going to last."

"Not knowing each other?" Elton stood up. "That's ridiculous. We've been married for twenty-four years!"

He turned away.

"Now, if you'll excuse me, I think I've had about all I can take for one day."

He felt her slip into bed some time later, but she was not there in the morning. He guessed she had put the coffee on and gone for an early jog. Elton pulled on some old clothes and a sweater and began raking leaves in the yard, taking his time, examining the eternally green grass, thick as a carpet. The sun fought off a cluster of low, black-bellied clouds, periodically breaking through. A street-sweeper lumbered by, brushes twirling, engine groaning. Anne appeared on the porch a half-hour later.

"Elton, Madge has called twice. You've had a number of important messages. And she wanted to remind you about lunch with some client from Virginia."

Elton carried on, dividing the lawn into sections, sweeping leaves into little piles.

"Elton, do you hear me?"

He turned, holding the rake like a hockey stick, his jaw jutting defiantly.

"I have four hundred and twenty-two days of accumulated sick leave. It is a matter of record."

He bent over, dug a stone out of the grass and tossed it into a hedge.

"That doesn't sound like you," Anne said.

Elton turned to her again.

"If you don't know me, how can you possibly stand there and say that's not like me?"

By the end of his statement he was pointing. They stared at each other in a silent standoff.

"I'm sorry," he said. "That was uncalled for." After a pause, "This isn't a time for talking. It's a time for thinking."

He left her standing on the porch and went back to his raking. He heard the door close, stood there for a minute doing nothing; then he went inside, noticing on the way that a brick in the first step had worked itself loose. Anne leaned against the kitchen counter with her back to him. He approached and gently placed his arms around her. She grasped one of his hands and held it tightly. The neighbor's collie had started barking about something, spoiling the quiet, but Elton ignored it.

"When I said it was a time for thinking, I meant that I'm just trying to make some logic out of all this, Annie."

"The walls of this house are papered with logic, Elton," she said, facing him.

He saw that she had been crying.

"It's feelings that are important. I want us to understand, to . . . to . . . oh, I don't know if anything I'm saying is making any sense."

He wrapped her in a full embrace.

"I know one thing," he said. "I can't make any sense out of any of this without you."

Elton called to inform the office he would not be in that day. Anne packed a lunch, and they drove to Green Lake. The food seemed to taste better in the open air. Little columns of steam spiraled up from the coffee. They flipped crusts to the ducks, then walked miles through neighboring Woodland Park, holding hands, talking, and reminiscing. He tried to remember the last time they had enjoyed such a day together. *It must have been years ago*, he thought. Elton breathed in gulps of the crisp air.

He wanted to go out for dinner, but at her insistence they

ate at home. Anne lit candles and played a favorite Vivaldi sonata on the stereo. To his great surprise, she mentioned a desire to accompany him to the Crusade meeting. He raised no objections, and they left together. She said nothing negative about the proceedings all evening. Elton noticed she sang out on the choruses, appearing even to enjoy herself. Afterward, they treated the Whartons to a late-night snack at one of Elton's favorite restaurants.

In bed that evening, Elton felt unusually talkative, carrying on, even when Anne barely acknowledged that she was listening.

"I don't know about you, but I've started to do some serious thinking about certain assumptions that I've left unchallenged for too long. Anne, I want your honest opinion on this. Do you think that I've . . . Anne?"

She had fallen asleep.

They slept late the next day and enjoyed a long, leisurely breakfast. Elton actually read some articles in the paper, instead of just examining them. Anne read an Ann Landers letter about a woman who discovered her husband painting his toenails. They both got a good laugh over it.

"Going back to work?" she asked.

"Why? You think I should?"

"I think so."

"I may," he said, "but I think I should pay someone an unexpected visit."

Elton kissed his wife and embarked on his first trip ever to Factorytown.

19

Greg's misgivings started the moment he hung up. Alone in Sheila's townhouse, he found it too easy to think. He accused himself of being reactionary and careless. His imagination ran wild with the mystery of the whole endeavor, and what might go wrong. A voice, soft and calm, and not unlike that of Elton, told him he had made a mistake. Sheila returned much earlier than he had expected, and he forgot the distress their dispute had caused.

His conscience pestered him. Two days later, he summoned the courage to call and back out. Tony barely let him talk, supplied him with directions and details, and repeatedly mentioned the money involved. Greg swallowed his objections and went along with an easy acquiesence that made him angry at himself. In disputes with Scott, he had often argued against what he perceived as "irrational" elements in the Christian faith. *And yet, he told himself, he had been swayed, not by anything reasonable, but by something he could not really define.* When he thought about it all sensibly, the voice of reason sounded a clear warning, and he had directly ignored it. Several times he attempted to make another call, but could not quite carry it through. He convinced himself that it might be too late for such a move. The night of the twenty-second came all too quickly. He made a pact with himself that this one night would be his first and last in Tony's employ.

Tony's attitude helped to ease his fears. He joked and laughed, as if he might be on some harmless errand for his parents, a mere trip to the store to buy bread. They drove north, past Everett, then down a windy road to a small wharf shared by a pair of tired trawlers and some pleasure craft. A lone gull flew circles above them. The sun sank down over the Olympic Mountains to the west. A light breeze blew off the water, bringing with it an invigorating salt smell. An old pickup truck with expired Oregon plates stood beside the boathouse, but nobody else was there. Tony did some investigating to make sure.

"Grab the poles," he urged Greg. "Maybe we'll do a little fishing while we're at it."

They carted the gear to the dock. Greg thought it was uncanny the way Tony seemed to automatically sense his reservations and offer defenses.

"The way I look at it," he said, "the way things are now is just like it was in the Prohibition times. Whatever the government does, people are still going to find a way to get what they want, right? What I am doing is providing a service for a product in demand."

"What exactly are we bringing in here? You never have told me, you know."

Tony dismissed the question with a gesture. "Somebody says something about abuse. Well, what can I do about that? Hey, I got no control over what people do with their own bodies. Look at bicycles. People get killed on bikes every day. Bikes are legal. Look at how many people drink themselves to death, like Cap's probably gonna do. And they not only sell booze but advertise it on television. Everybody's such hypocrites."

"I know, but . . ."

"But what?"

"I don't know. Look, after tonight, I want to cut loose."

"I won't need you after tonight. I might try a different line of business myself. I don't need this any more. Hey, relax, man. Don't get your shorts in a knot. It's a piece of cake."

Their small boat was still at the dock. Tony ran a quick check over all the equipment, consulting his watch every few minutes. He scanned the horizon with a pair of binoculars. Before they shoved off, Tony, in plain sight, shoved an automatic pistol into his belt. He saw the way Greg looked at it.

"Just for the sake of argument," he said.

Greg felt a kind of heat rise within him, accompanied by a desperate urge to break free and run.

"Hey, don't look so nervous. Be cool. You're never gonna win this much money unless you take the U. S. Open. And even then you'll have to work harder."

Tony fired up the outboard. The boat lurched into open water, severing the last route of escape. He kept it at full throttle for about ten minutes, then slowed. A thick womb of blackness gradually enveloped the craft. They bobbed up and down slowly on gentle swells.

"How we going to find anything out here?"

"With a little help from some of the miracles of modern technology."

By the light of a lantern, Tony showed Greg how to use the sonar depth finder. Greg hung over the bow and gave readings.

"I still don't see how we are going to do it."

"It's a deep, dark secret. A trick of the trade. Just give me the readings. Make sure you keep the lantern low."

They putted along as if trolling for gamefish.

"What's the count now?"

"Seven. Are you sure . . . ?"

"We're going for ten. Just keep it low. That's it. I think we're close."

They seemed to be staying in one spot. Greg's back was sore from leaning close to the water. He shivered with the chill, even though the wind had dropped. A tiny, white marker drifted into the circle of light thrown by the lantern.

"There it is!"

Tony steered toward it. They began to drag in a series of plastic-wrapped white packets.

"You just hooked yourself a brand new Porsche, pal."

Tony's face, though swathed in shadows, bore an expression bordering on reverence, like a movie pirate who pries open the treasure chest. He took a quick inventory.

"Shouldn't we get out of here?"

"Just making sure it is all here. See anything else?"

Greg stood and held the lantern high. A loud, whooping siren came out of nowhere, followed by a searchlight. Powerful engines started up, not too distant, he guessed from the sound.

"Patrol!" Their boat faced the intruding vessel. Tony swore and gunned the motor; his tight turn catapulted Greg into the water.

He tried to yell but only filled his mouth with water. The weight of his clothing pulled him under, where he could hear the pulse of the approaching patrol boat, His limbs, seized with the cold, at first refused to move. He kicked his legs wildly, trying to stay in motion. His breathing was forced and erratic.

The light of the patrol boat scoured the darkness for Tony, who took evasive action, steering in zig-zag patterns. Greg was between the two vessels. The patrol boat bore down on him. He tried to swim out of the way, but his joints seemed to have locked up. He ducked underwater. The engine noise thundered in his ears. Everything was black. The hull crashed into his right shoulder. Lights exploded in his head. A pain shot through his upper body. His lungs pleaded for air, and he worked his way to the surface. *They must have felt the impact,* he thought. He *wanted* them to pick him up, whatever the consequences. But the patrol boat sped past him. He yelled instinctively, but it was futile.

The clothing now seemed to weigh tons. It dragged and

pulled on him like some huge fist. The injured right arm began to throb, sending jolts of pain through his body. He thrashed around in an awkward side-stroke, discovering, when his energy had abated, that he could remain afloat by turning on his back and using a frog-style kick.

A loud babble of voices ran out of control in his mind. He heard echoing, reverberating laughter. Bits of conversation came back to him, lines from sermons, stray phrases, forgotten images. "You will die," he heard a voice say. "I will die, Thoreau is already dead." *Was it true?* he insanely asked himself. Was Thoreau dead? "All of us will die," came the voice again. He imagined himself sinking into the bottomless deep, downward forever, and out of existence. A set of swells from a distant freighter washed over him. The frequency and strength of his kicks had severely diminished. He found himself calling out, the energy flowing from some untapped source. He half-heard himself yell, "No!" as if directly addressing Death itself. He called on God, on Elton, on Scott, on Jesus, on Reverend Keith Wharton and his wife. It occurred to him that he might be moving the wrong way, or not going anywhere at all, and he renewed his cries, sounding like a wounded animal.

He tried to float and rest, but a leg began to cramp. Every movement, every kick, took all his strength. His cries of *Oh, God!* grew fainter. He passed into a kind of trance, managing, by some process, to keep moving. He bumped into something. It was a piece of driftwood, too small to help him stay afloat. The coldness of the water numbed everything but his face, and he sensed a series of tingles. He maintained an almost hypnotic rhythm: *kick, rest, breathe; kick, rest, breathe.* After a long, black, undefined space of time, his foot struck something. He groped around with his toes. A swell swept him along another few feet. He felt the bottom. Pressing even his injured right arm into service, he fought toward the shore with the instinct of a salmon. When he could stand with both feet in place, he stood there a moment, discovering himself breathing a prayer of thanks, possessed with the intoxicating sureness of life and survival. Another wave inundated him. He slogged along, the water growing shallower. Straining his ears, he heard the welcome slap of waves on a shore, followed by the churning of stones. In knee-deep water, he stumbled and plunged in again. His right shoulder seared him with pain. Once on shore, he fell on his face and collapsed with exhaustion.

His next conscious sensation was something rough in his mouth. Tiny particles of sand ground against his teeth. He opened his eyes. It was light. He was staring into the beach, a bottle cap lay a few inches from his nose. He felt immediately afraid; his body shivering. He tried to move before somebody saw him.

The shoulder! It felt as if torn from his body. His hands, he noticed, slightly terrified, were a bright bluish-purple. He managed to stand, turning to look at the body of water out of which he had emerged alive by some undeniable miracle. The surface lay flat, sparkling with the morning sunshine. He sat down on a log and let the rays warm him. A deep thankfulness crowded out his troubled thoughts.

He got his bearings, found the nearest road and began to hitchhike. Three cars passed, the drivers looking at him horrified. A van pulled over. Greg got in. The driver's beard covered almost his entire face, his large nostrils two caverns amidst a forest.

"Man, what happened to you?"

"It's a long story."

Greg nodded off to sleep, leaning his head against the window. As they entered Seattle, the man poked Greg awake.

"You want to go to a hospital or something?" the driver asked.

Fear rose in Greg's throat. He noticed the ashtray, overflowing with twisted cigarette butts.

"No, I'm okay. Listen," he gave Sheila's address. "Is it out of your way?"

"It is, but I'll take you there. Man, you are in bad shape."

"God bless you, man." Greg said when he dropped him off, surprising himself.

Nobody was home at Sheila's. He discarded the soggy clothing and stood in front of a heater duct with the temperature on full blast. Dry garments made him feel unbelievably wonderful, almost a human being again. Turning to the kitchen, he gulped food like an animal, washing it down with a pot of coffee. This done, he built a fire, wrapped himself in blankets and fell asleep right in front of the hearth, waking just after noon.

The shoulder would have to be attended to. He dialed Sheila's physician and told him he had to see him right away. On the way, he invented a story about how he had been injured. The doctor seemed to disbelieve him but said nothing. Greg was told he had a shoulder separation, and that he would have to wear a sling. He put it on with little hesitancy, knowing he would have lots of explaining to do, in any case.

The late afternoon hours dragged. He wondered if Sheila might not have taken off for a few days out of spite, when he failed to come home the previous night. His mind rehearsed all kinds of scenarios. When the Porsche pulled up, his innards felt coiled into a spring.

Her initial expression was one of disbelief. Then, quickly, her face darkened, and she began to speak through her teeth. She asked what had happened, exploding in rage when he had barely started his answer. She swore loudly and eloquently, clearly enunciating the consonants at the end of her four-letter words. Pacing around, she heaped abuse on him, finally calming enough to organize a coherent statement.

"I set you up for the kind of success that only the select even fantasize about, and you go and ruin it like some self-destructive imbecile."

"Sheila, let's not get carried away. So, I miss one tournament. People get hurt all the time. It's the way of the world."

"Not my world. Look at you. You're broken equipment,

Greg. Those kinds of injuries never heal the same. You might as well face the fact that you'll probably be second-rate."

"Thanks. I really need all that encouragement. Look, let's stop yelling at each other, sit down and take a look at the facts. Why should we let one incident . . ."

"*Why*?" she asked, brows arched, eyes bulging, hands on her hips. "Because what I want is a winner, not some reclamation project."

He knew it was over.

"Do clear your things out," she said, suddenly calm, in the same voice she used with waiters. "When I come back, I want everything gone."

Greg experienced a vivid hallucination of himself, smacking her across the face. Scores of insults rushed to his lips, but no further. She stood in the doorway, looking at him as if he might have some rare, infectious disease. She started to say something, but just shook her head with a sarcastic expression on her face. He thought this twice as bad as anything she had done so far.

She slammed the door and drove off with a squeal of tires. Weak of body, wounded in mind, Greg dredged up the courage to call his brother. Dialing the number required a tremendous act of the will.

"You want *me* to come *there*?"

"You have to come. I'll explain when you get here."

There was silence at the other end, as if Scott considered the possibility of a crank call.

"Will you come, *please*?" Greg weakly added.

"Be right there."

While he and Scott packed up his things, Greg explained. Scott listened attentively, probing. Greg felt a strange compulsion to tell all, and did so. As they drove off, Scott unloaded on him.

"Anything and everything as long as you come in first, right? What's it going to be next? I hear there's big bucks in kiddie porn. Maybe you can sell it down by the bus stop, or at the local schoolyard."

"What do you want from me? Sackcloth and ashes?"

"What do I want? Look at you. You risk jail—and even your life—just to impress some people you thought were your friends. Has it ever occurred to you that you could very well be dead now?"

Greg stared straight ahead.

"You could be gone," Scott continued, "and we'd never know."

Greg rejected an insurgent protest.

"You know," Scott said, "I never realized until this moment how little any of us mean to you."

The words pierced what was left of his armor. They drove the rest of the way to Factorytown in silence. Scott called Laura to come over, and together they carried his belongings up to the apartment. They then left Greg alone while they attended a function at school. Greg felt as if in confinement. A couple in the flat above shrieked at each other. The dripping faucet grated his nerves, like fingers dragged across a blackboard. He sat and stared out the window for hours. A liquor-store light blinked on and off, on and off. It's message read like a cruel joke:

IT'S THE WATER

20

WHERE A MAN BELONGS

The billboard showed a lean, tanned man rafting a wild river, cigarette firmly in place between teeth. Winds had torn loose the corner of another sign for a Canadian whiskey. This sported an elegant woman in a full-length evening gown, her smiling face bearing the promise of ecstasy.

Elton felt somehow that he should have to drive farther to visit his son. The rougher neighborhoods were closer than he had remembered. They began abruptly, almost as if there were an invisible line of division. There were no shopping malls, and few grocery stores, though every corner seemed to have a Mom-and-Pop-style market and a coin-operated laundry. The low, red brick buildings seemed all the same with their old swinging signs, crumbling parapet walls and barred windows. He drove by a theater.

THIS WEEK ONLY: KUNG FU MOVIES
FEATURING BRUCE LEE

NEXT—RICHARD PRYOR LIVE
ON SUNSET STRIP

A wizened oriental woman crossed slowly in front of him at a traffic light. Somebody in a foreign sports car honked at her, then rolled down the window and yelled when she did not speed up. Elton noticed that all three public telephones along that block were in use. An old man swigged off a bottle in a paper bag. The wind blew papers around in the gutter. The gray sky cast a pall over everything.

He had some trouble finding Scott's apartment; someone had crashed into a sign, rendering it useless for directions. The streets were lined with cars. He drove slowly, watching for the familiar Land Cruiser. A sign loomed, half-covered with spray-painted graffiti.

CRIMINAL BEWARE!

Neighborhood Watch in effect. All suspicious behavior will be immediately reported to Seattle Police.

The apartments, too, all looked the same; shabby walkups, their porches crowded with bicycles, dogs, toys, and junk. Elton finally located Scott's flat, and a parking space some hundred yards off. He had difficulty wedging his Buick into the small space and angered himself by bumping his wheel against the curb, a habit for which he had often chided his wife. A rusty Oldsmobile in front of the building stood with its hood open and engine removed. A stripped cylinder head and empty beer bottle lay beneath it, a valve cover lay upside down in front, half-full of water. The ground in the yard was free from grass, and soft from the rains. A sparrow splashed in a puddle.

"Do you want to buy something?"

The voice spun Elton around. A black youth with food smeared on his shirt stood at the corner, displaying various gadgets and tools which Elton immediately suspected he had stolen.

"Do you live in this building?"

The child looked afraid but nodded.

"Do you know if Scott Stuart lives here?"

The boy regarded him with one eye closed. Elton expected a smart answer.

"He lives here, but he can't talk now."

Elton wondered momentarily if Scott had instructed the lad to run interference for him.

"And why might it be that he can't talk now? Could you tell me that, please?"

"He's reading a book."

"Oh, I see. He's reading a book. That sounds like Scott all right. Well, I think he might be able to spare me a few minutes at least. You see, I'm his father."

Startled, the boy looked him up and down for a few seconds then said, "Well, okay." He pointed. "He's up there. In the back. Number five."

"Thank you, young man."

Elton wiped the mud from his shoes on the first step, then started up the stairway, tensing at the way it creaked, as if it might instantly collapse. A woman in a white uniform on the way down passed him without a word or any eye contact. Elton turned and watched her give a house key and a series of instructions to the child. She shot Elton a wary glance before leaving. Her old Ford backfired and blew out blue smoke. Elton kept going up the steps. The upper porch was covered with little circles where someone had been bouncing a ball. Noises of a television game show from another apartment distracted him. He knocked at door number 5.

Out of the corner of his eye, he saw the chintz curtains part. Fingers fumbled with a deadbolt and safety chain. The door swung open. Scott stood there in worn corduroy pants and a University of Washington jersey bearing the number

25. His face looked tired, especially the eyes. He had the overall appearance of someone slipping into middle age, not a seminary student. A bare toe poked out of one sock.

Scott was surprised. He thought it might be Greg, who had gone to the tennis club to pick up his things. "Come on in, Dad."

Elton peered around as if he had mistakenly strayed into a room full of abstract paintings. The light switches were all missing their plastic backup plates. The floors seemed out of level, the walls slightly awry. Paint on the ceiling flaked and curled into shapes like potato chips. He heard the faucet dripping, and sniffed an odor reminiscent of burnt toast and soggy coffee grounds.

"Here, have a seat."

"Thank you. You certainly have a lot of books down here. You are building quite a library."

Elton reclined in one of the folding chairs. The legs varied in length, and the chair rocked when he shifted his weight.

"I confess. It's my worst vice."

"What's that you're reading?"

"It's Sider's *Rich Christians in an Age of Hunger.*"

"And how are your studies coming along?"

"Fine. Some of the courses aren't horribly relevant, but that's to be expected, I suppose." Then Scott asked, "How's the corporate world doing?"

"Oh, same old rat race."

Elton stood up and slowly turned a full circle, examining everything again. He backed off a few steps.

"Something wrong, Dad?"

"You know," he said after a pause, "it's curious how angry I feel just *seeing* you here."

Elton thrust his hands into his coat pockets.

"All my life," he continued, looking down at a small clod of mud, still clinging to one shoe, "I've worked to get ahead. I've struggled for status in the company for myself and for my family. I've put everything aside to make a better life for all of us. And now you are here as a kind of, well, social descender for want of a better term. It was something I just was not prepared for."

He glanced around again; then looked out the window, noticing the smoke billowing up from the mill. His mind wandered to an abstraction, then back to his train of thought. Scott sat attentively, listening.

"But lately, it seems that in my own life, every choice I've made, no matter how carefully I've made it, somebody always winds up getting hurt."

"Maybe there aren't any safe choices, Dad."

Elton shifted to a more erect posture, and trained his eyes on Scott.

"I want you to tell me something. What does this place, this sort of thing you are doing, have to offer to someone of your potential?"

Scott started to say something, but held back, as though a reply would serve no purpose.

"You don't honestly think that you are singlehandedly going to expunge poverty from the earth do you? My goodness, Scott, the only budgets in the world higher than our national welfare budget are the entire budgets of the United States and the entire budgets of the Soviet Union. It's not as if there is nothing being done. We've thrown money at the problem for years, and it is still with us and always will be. Wasn't it Jesus who said that the poor are with you always?"

"But, Dad, everybody's with us." Scott said, his voice cracking. "All the more reason to be down here for these people."

Scott appeared at the point of breaking into tears.

"I want to live it out. All of it. Dad, I don't think any amount of arguing is going to convince you of that. It's what I want to do. It's not a question of what this place has to offer *me.* You've got it backwards. It's what *I* have to offer, and I can't offer only words and panaceas, then run back to my nice WASP ghetto. I *have* to be here. I wish you could understand that."

Elton sagged noticeably, as if accepting a rebuke. He lowered his voice.

"You know, your brother accused me of not being truly Christian." He dropped Scott's gaze, then met it again. "Would you concur with that?"

The question brought a look of pain to Scott, as if he would do anything to avoid answering.

"I don't know," he managed with difficulty, then repeated himself after thinking for another moment. "I hope so," he said finally, "I mean, I hope that you are."

Elton sat down again. He grappled for something to say, his mind a jumble of questions, confessions, and defenses. He shook off a strong urge to make an incoherent outburst, and swallowed a lump in his throat.

"You, want some coffee or something, Dad?"

"Thank you, but I think I should be getting along. Is there . . . anything you need?"

"Not that I can think of right at the moment, other than that I'd like you to stop by again."

"You'd really like me to?"

"Of course I would. Come anytime."

"Thank you, son," Elton said, feeling slightly disoriented, "I may just do that."

At the bottom of the stairs, he remembered some other things he had wanted to say, and ask. He thought of going back up. The black child appeared out of nowhere, both knees covered with mud. Elton noticed his shoes had no laces.

"Did he talk to you?"

"Yes, he certainly did."

A trio of youths lurked near Elton's car, fleeing at his approach. He gave the vehicle a thorough check, finding that nothing had been touched, but noticing a rough smear on the tire where he had brushed the curb.

Heading for work, he began thinking of the backlog of work that awaited him—the calls, the appointments, the underlings in need of his wisdom, the papers needing his signature. He debated the best way to handle it all. Thus occupied, he promptly forgot the morning's conversation with his son.

The problems exceeded his expectations. He felt like a broken-field runner, avoiding tackles from all sides, as well as from behind. The client from Virginia expressed his displeasure over Elton's non-appearance at their scheduled meeting and threatened to cancel their business deal. Marshaling all his powers of persuasion, Elton apologized and managed to persuade him otherwise. All day Elton became evasive when anyone probed, however gently, if anything might be wrong. On the way home, he passed a garbage truck and experienced a strange admiration for the men on it. They came to work, did their job, returned home in the afternoon without the slightest thought or care of what had happened that day. Entering his driveway, he questioned the value of his own calling. It was not a job to leave at the door.

In a corner of the living room, Anne unveiled the roll-top desk, glistening with the new finish.

"It's beautiful," he said, passing a hand over it. "They just don't make things like that any more."

"Did you see Scott?"

"I did."

"And?"

"Well, the place is worse than you could possibly imagine. You'd almost think they were in the middle of demolition. I don't know, maybe it was my revulsion with the place, but for a while I felt at a distinct loss for what to say. It's obvious that nothing either you or I say to him can deter him from staying down there."

"Was that all you talked about?"

"No. I remembered everything Greg said that night he came in drunk, how he accused me of not being Christian. I asked Scott if he would agree with that statement."

"Elton, sometimes I really think you are far too hard on yourself."

"You know, I thought for a moment he was never going to get his answer out. He seemed to be struggling so hard, I almost expected some sort of outburst."

"What did he say? I mean, about you being a Christian."

Elton shifted over to the end of the couch. He crossed his legs and placed them on the coffee table; then he leaned his head back and stared at the ceiling. He let out a long breath. Anne sat beside him, taking his hand.

"If you don't want to tell me, that's fine."

"He said. 'I hope you are a Christian.'"

"Oh, Elton."

He put an arm around her. Neither spoke for a long time.

"What do you think I am?" he asked.

21

Greg slept in late, alone in the chilly apartment, wrapped in a warm cocoon of blankets. He lay there in a nether world of half-slumber, faintly aware of the burgeoning light and stray noises from outside; temporarily at peace, with no desire to move; imagining that his sole function was to hold the couch in place by his weight. A drumming, thumping tattoo on the porch outside sprung open his eyes. He jerked himself up, threw on a heavy shirt, and cracked the door open, addressing the offender in a snarl.

"Hey! What do you think this is? Don't you know people are sleeping in here? Why aren't you in school, kid? Now get that ball out of here."

Oliver beat a hasty retreat inside, without so much as another dribble. Greg slammed the door.

"Little pest," he muttered.

Cold air seemed to ooze in through the very walls. Greg fiddled with the heater, managing to coax some life out of it. The shower was defective, so he ran a bath, the water barely

165

above lukewarm even when turned solely on hot. He lathered with a sliver of soap, careful not to aggravate the shoulder, which had improved, but still gave him pain. He dressed and put on the sling.

The pilot light on the stove had gone out, so he struck a match. The blue flames flared out, forming a little flower of heat and light on which he set the kettle. There was plenty of instant coffee, but, he discovered, no sugar, and only a dribble of milk. Black, the stuff tasted like acid. He endured a few sips and dumped the remainder down the drain.

Boredom settled on him like dust, bringing a kind of paralysis. Little of Scott's reading material held any interest. He flipped through a book *Simple Life: The Christian Stance Toward Possessions*, noting scribbled comments in the margins. The other volume about the cult of narcissism that Scott hinted he "should read" he avoided entirely. Foraging through the periodicals, he found an old issue of *Esquire*, discovering that Scott had cut out some pages, including the last section of the article he attempted to read. Greg tossed the magazine aside and turned on the radio loud enough to drown out the television noises from next door. A disc jockey touted an upcoming rock concert. *Live at the Kingdome. Five of the most important musicians of our time! Ticket prices start at ten dollars. Don't miss it!* A song he despised came on, so he kept changing stations, eventually shutting it off. A gentle rain started to fall. He considered going next door and telling them to turn down the television. The synthetic laughter was maddening, as though it might be a taunt directed at him. He pulled on a jacket. The phone rang as his hand touched the door.

Someone responded to the newspaper ad he had placed for the Triumph. He had trouble believing it at first. They sounded interested.

"We'll be right down to take a look," a filtered gravelly voice said.

The thought of having a sizable chunk of money at his disposal excited him. He dropped the plans to confront the neighbors and attended to the bike, at the side of the building under a covering of green plastic garbage bags. It started after three or four kicks, and he let it run, warming the engine. Two men in their early thirties pulled up in a black van. Each wore a small earring. They checked the bike over; one of them drove it around the block.

"It seems to miss a bit."

"Needs a tune up, that's all," Greg replied. "I just haven't had the money."

"Take five bills for it?"

"I really have to get six. I put two new tires on it. Had the valves done, too."

"How about five fifty?"

Greg affected deep indecision, but had already made up his mind. "Let's go for it," he said. They startled him by counting out five crisp hundred dollar bills and one fifty from a trucker's wallet and then pressed them into his willing hands.

"Don't kill yourself on it," Greg said as they loaded it up with a series of grunts.

"Is that what you tried to do?" one of them asked, alluding to his sling.

"No, that was something else."

A flash of nostalgia for the bike quickly abated. The corner store would not accept the large bills, so he walked four blocks to the nearest bank and opened an account. On the way back, he bought all the groceries he could carry, and fixed a hefty meal of eggs, bacon, toast, and coffee. He felt so good about his stroke of fortune that he did the dishes and cleaned up the apartment, leaving soon after to celebrate.

By the second week, Greg established a pattern, sleeping in as late as possible, then departing to some favorite bars. The retreat to the dark, noisy, smoke-filled caverns became automatic, like a badger returning to its hole. He found plenty of company; the places teemed with laid-off workers from Boeing and the various forest-industry plants. When swapping hardship stories with them, he told numerous lies, reasoning that they would think his real story the biggest lie of all. He played pool and darts, drank his share, flirted with barmaids and spent money abundantly. On one occasion, when well into his cups, he shared a series of pitchers with a woman who invited him over to her place. He went along. Outside, in the light, he saw she was much older, probably in her forties. She was slightly cross-eyed, with a face painted like a whore, and bearing a sluttish expression, emphasized by the way she chewed her gum and dragged on a cigarette. She had looked so different inside. Greg made some feeble excuses that he had forgotten to perform some important task, then fled around the corner into another bar. He drank alone, his mind swamped with thoughts of Sheila, the accident, and the course of his life. It left a bitter taste, and he was unable to sweep it all away. A jukebox cranked out tear-jerking country- and western-love songs.

More than once, Scott had to retrieve him at closing time. He expected a scolding on each occasion, but Scott dutifully escorted him home without any sermon. Greg could not deal with this, and found that it angered him. He wanted to argue and defend himself, to accuse Scott of being a self-righteous Puritan, but Scott never gave him the opportunity and refused to be baited, however snide Greg was in his remarks or loutish in manner.

Greg attempted to stay home on a Monday, a tiny stab at reform, but heard a radio announcement that the football game at the Kingdome was a sellout, and would be televised locally on *Monday Night Football*. He capitulated and headed to The Norwester, a popular singles bar with a giant television screen.

He arrived early, before all the working people, and garnered a good seat. He lost count of the pitchers he consumed and the rounds he bought. A sloe-eyed waitress with turquoise bracelets seemed to take a liking to him. She became friendlier with every tip, but left at half-time with a tall, black man, whose muscles bulged through his jacket.

Cosell's visage and comments drew hoots of derision.

Somebody chucked a peanut at the screen and was promptly ejected without a struggle by a three-hundred-pound
bouncer. The place rang with whistles and cheers at every
good play by the Seahawks. The local squad drew even, but
the quarterback was sacked and coughed up the ball. Two
plays later, the opposition placekicker calmly kicked a field
goal to win the game in the closing seconds. The bar quieted
down; people left in droves.

Greg checked his funds and found them dwindling. He
left The Norwester and went to a dumpier place, where the
waitresses were old but beer was cheap. He drank and played
pool with some fishermen, frittering away the rest of his money. Just after eleven, he saw his brother wading through the
smoke that hung in the air like fog, and whose odor had pen-
etrated the very woodwork.

Scott looked angry, as though thoroughly tired of the
whole routine. His mouth formed a tight, horizontal line.

"Let's go."

Greg looked up at him. "You twenty-one? I'm going to
have to see some identification."

Greg's drinking mates looked puzzled. One of them said,
"New in town, sailor?" then broke into riotous laughter at his
own joke. Greg joined him.

"This man," he said, gesturing to his brother, "is the
Robin Hood of Factorytown. God sendeth him to protect the
downtrodden masses against the evil landlords."

"Let's go, Greg."

"I once suggested to him that we rob the rich *and* the
poor and split it three ways, but he wouldn't go for it. Ha! Ha!"

"Greg ..."

"All right, all right," Greg whined, when he had recovered
from a fit of laughter. "I'm going."

"You're drunk," Scott said, when they got out in the
street, where a sign read:

RIDICULE IS THE ARGUMENT OF FOOLS

Greg pondered it for a moment, as though it might be

some profound maxim. He sensed a surge of alcoholized eloquence.

"Drunk? That's certainly an astute observation."

"Just what do you think you are trying to do?"

He stumbled and brushed against a newspaper box, sending a quick jolt of pain up his arm.

"Well, in highly technical language, I think I'm trying to destroy myself." He felt himself almost lucid for an instant and added in a normal voice, "I can't imagine why, though."

Scott attempted to help him walk properly. Greg angrily shook him off.

"Don't touch me!"

"I'm just trying to keep you from falling on your drunken face, which is a distinct possibility at this point."

"Okay, okay. Don' whip me, massa."

The evening air acted like a smelling salt, and Greg began to make better progress. Nearing the apartment, three dark figures emerged from an alley and blocked their path. Greg felt himself seized with fear. The trio suddenly rushed them. Scott seemed to be their target, and Greg made an awkward lunge in his brother's defense. One of the attackers swept him aside, dealing Greg a pair of jabs to the face and a stiff right to the midsection. He landed on the pavement like a splattered egg.

"Run, Greg!"

Doubled over with pain, Greg watched the three of them bludgeon his brother with fists and feet. He heard the sickening sound of the impact, the sharp cries of pain, the oaths and insults that were spit, not spoken. Time seemed suspended, his vision blurred. He saw Scott writhing to avoid blows, succeeding only in drawing more. Greg sensed a bitter, utter helplessness. He tried, mentally, to divert the attack to himself. They were almost finished now. Two of them fled. One remained, drew back a booted foot and drove it into Scott's groin before running off with the others. Scott tried valiantly to stand, but collapsed into the gutter, landing in a fetal position.

Greg dragged himself up. He hunched over his brother in a state of shock, breathing in quick spurts, wondering if Scott might be dead, and blaming himself. He closed his eyes, threw his head back, and howled.

Some neighbors Scott had visited with the leaflets helped them back to the apartment. Greg summoned Mrs. Robinson, who leaped into action with the cool efficiency of a surgeon, dispatching Oliver for bandages and disinfectant. Laura arrived on the scene and pitched in. Her eyes shone with tears.

"Is he going to be all right, Mom?" Oliver queried.

"He'll be okay. This is their way of telling him not to play in their yard." She looked over at Laura. "I told him I could see it coming. You've got one stubborn boyfriend here. The landlord's boys don't play high-school games."

Greg shut himself in the bathroom, possessed of a torrent of sorrow, unlike anything he had ever experienced. He visualized his brother lying injured. His mind kept repeating, *It's my fault. I'm sorry if I hurt you.* The lingering aftertaste of violence raised the specter of Death and took him back to the night in the water, when some secret door had been opened, enabling him to call on God as naturally as he struggled to stay above water. He sensed an urge to do so again, but for different reasons. He remained in exile in the tiny room long after Scott was patched up and coherent again.

"I'm sorry," Greg told him, finally emerging. Scott managed a weak smile and tried to go to sleep.

"You were right," Greg went on, determined to talk to the exhausted Scott. "I was within a hair of losing it out there. Don't know how I ended up on the beach . . . just starting to go under and yelling for God as naturally . . . as breathing! It's almost as if death is some kind of a secret. You are so helpless." There was silence in the room. Greg continued, "It's always been natural to you, bro. I've envied that. You always knew you needed Him. You've always known . . . guess I kept figuring there was plenty of time. You had enough for both of us."

Greg stared at the ceiling, sure now that Scott was asleep, but glad he had finally voiced how he really felt. That night, Greg's turbulent dreams refused to let him sleep. His mind replayed the violence. He saw a frightening vision of himself stumbling down the street; suddenly old and decrepit; his face etched with lines; mouth slobbering; mucus smeared on his sleeve; shoes cracked; a bottle in his pocket. By morning he felt barely human, broken.

22

A spider spun a network of threads around the light bulb in the middle of Scott's living room. While Greg watched, it lowered itself toward the floor for no apparent reason. Greg wondered what it would be like to act out of pure instinct—to be blissfully unaware of one's own existence. He even envied the creature dangling in midair by a thread.

It was raining again, trapping him inside the apartment that grew more oppressive with each passing minute. Laura had lent him her portable television. He watched a creaking old Elvis Presley picture to divert his mind. There were fights in it. *Very different,* he thought, *from the genuine article I recently experienced.* Nobody seemed to bleed, or even have their hair overly ruffled.

"Are you confused?" came a voice during a commercial break. "Are you uncertain what you want out of life? Are you stuck in some kind of a dead-end job, or have you been laid off your previous job?"

The announcer's eyes flicked back and forth to the

teleprompter. He sat behind an expensive desk, pointing a finger at his audience.

"Now, you, yes, you, can learn to drive the big rigs at Northwest School of Truck Driving. You can make big money and be financially independent. Call this number today. It's your key to success."

Similar commercials came on for a computer-repair institute, a bank-teller training program, and a bartenders' school. *Do you know where your life is going?* they all asked.

Greg stuck with the film until the end. The hero vanquished his enemies, won the race, and drove triumphantly away in a new car with a beautiful girl by his side and a trophy in the back seat. Nobody questioned their role. Nobody died. Everything was safe and happy forever. Another talking head, this time a woman, addressed him.

"Are you dissatisfied with ... ?"

He snapped the set off.

Greg counted his money. At least, he told himself, he had not squandered all, even though the majority of it was forever gone. He watched for the mailman, expecting his overdue last check from the tennis club, but all the letters were for Scott. The rain failed to let up, so he donned a hooded jacket, ran out and bought an evening paper. A soggy mongrel dog with a pink nose scooted past him up the stairs on the way back. He checked the time and threw some frozen dinners into the oven, so they would be ready when Scott returned home.

"I was wondering," Greg asked his brother over dinner, "if I might borrow your car tomorrow."

Scott kept his eyes on his plate at first and continued chewing. His face was patched with shiny purple-black bruises and his nose looked slightly askew. He looked at Greg, as though he might be assessing a job applicant, eyes penetrating, searching for motives.

"Maybe," he said. "What do you want it for?"

"Well, I want to kind of get away for a day. I don't know, I have some serious thinking to do. I find it hard to think around here."

"Have you been reading Aristotle?"

"No, why?"

"He's the one who said the unexamined life is not worth living."

"I just want to get away by myself for a while. I'm going to have to make some kind of move pretty soon, some important decisions."

"Your shoulder feeling better?"

Greg nodded. "Look, I'm imposing on you here. I just want to put a little distance between myself and this place. You know it's hard to be in here all day."

"True."

Scott speared a green bean with his fork, popped it in his mouth, and washed it down with some milk.

"Okay, you can use it." A grin spread across Scott's face. "But only if you stay away from Canada and Mexico."

The next morning, Greg drove Scott and Laura to school. They got into a discussion about the similarities between the people of Jim Jones' Guyana colony and certain groups of Moslem fundamentalists. Laura discoursed on the differences between Christianity and traditional religion, but they arrived before she could finish. Scott got out, put a hand on the door and said to Greg, "I hope you find whatever it is you are looking for."

Greg drove first to Capitol Hill. He made one pass of his parents' house, which looked as majestic as ever. Several blocks away, children filed into the school he once attended. He watched them swinging their lunch boxes, jumping, and running about like young deer. An electric bell clanged, and they swarmed toward the door, leaving the yard empty. He passed on to the high school.

Students gathered in clusters, many dressed so similar as to constitute a uniform, but a few in outrageous punk chic, with mohawk haircuts amd mirror sunglasses. They laughed and smoked cigarettes, faces glib, confident. Greg remembered his days there, recognizing himself among them. He tried to think of one thing he had learned in its confines that would help him answer the questions that so troubled him. He thought, too, of the stages of life, each clearly marked with a ceremony, like graduation, with no possibility of retreat once a certain level had been attained.

He turned down the idea of wandering around the University. His memories of that institution were fresh, and the traffic there was always chaotic. An urge to revisit the island possessed him. He yielded to it.

Driving north out of the city, he thought it would be so very easy to do what Scott had forbidden, and just flee as far as possible. On examination, however, such a scheme collapsed into hopeless unrealities, and he rejected it. He rolled down the window and breathed in the air, eyes feasting on the majestic scenery. The old car hurtled him onward to the ferry. A lonesome truck driver talked at him all the way across.

Greg stopped for food at the island store. The old man did not recognize him at first.

"Remember? I cut a cord of wood for you once. You paid me in canned goods."

"Sure," he said on further inspection, "I remember. You looked a little different then, if I recall right. A little on the woolly side. Sure, I remember you. Say, there was a fellow looking for you a while back. Said he was your brother."

"He found me."

"What are you doing out here this time? I don't know anybody that needs any wood cut right now."

"Just visiting," Greg said. "Just having a look around."

"You going out to that island?"

Greg nodded.

"Remember," the proprietor told him as he left, "nobody's supposed to be out there this time a year you know."

"I know," Greg told him. "I know."

He bought a quart of orangeade and a bag of peanuts

and took them with him.

The attendant at the boat rental appeared puzzled at the way Greg stood rigidly on the dock, staring at the skiff, hesitant to get in.

"Is there something wrong? You afraid?" he asked.

"No," Greg said. "Nothing's wrong. I was just thinking of something."

He crossed the bow of a ketch on the way over, waving to the man at the wheel. The captain doffed his hat and waved back. A woman fished off the stern below a fluttering Canadian flag, a little patch of red and white against the sky. He read the name of the vessel, written in a neat arc above the home port:

WANDERESS
VICTORIA

For a moment, he fantasized far-away places. How convenient to be able to set sail at will.

The paths on the island did not appear to have been recently used. Everything was lush and wet. Moss spread up the trees like green velvet. He plucked a toad stool some eight inches across. Someone had, he felt certain, visited his former homesite, possibly even squatted there for a few nights. Cans and debris lay strewn about, a wine bottle, some empty .22 shells, a wilted magazine. The pole bearing his carved eagle tilted to one side, as though the bird had been shot and plummeted toward the earth. As he had done at the schools, Greg replayed the scenes of his life there: the time with Ursula; the chill, starry nights; the fires; eating out of cans; the visit of his brother. It, too, seemed a lost epoch, never to relived. Sitting in a patch of weak sunlight, he mused on the impermanence and frailty of everything. Nothing stayed the same. Everything got old, withered, died. An unidentified animal rushed through the bush, startling him. He closed his eyes and remained still, listening to the varied sounds of the forest; birds singing, leaves rustling; a faint swish of waves in the distance. Looking up, billowy clouds appeared to have the shape of a lion's mane. A line of Thoreau worked its way into his mind: *I left the woods for as good a reason as I went there. Perhaps I had other lives to live, and could not spare any more time for that one.* He left earlier than he had planned, walking directly back to the boat. Once under way, he remembered the clandestine marijuana patch, and thought about turning back—but did not.

For a reason he did not entirely understand, Greg drove to the beach on which he had washed up like some latter-day Jonah. Standing there and looking out at the horizon, he heard again the thunder of the boat engines followed by the crunching thud and explosion of pain. He pictured himself floundering in the wet blackness, calling out to the God whose presence he had steadfastly avoided, and finding himself alive as one from the dead the next morning. He discovered himself actually shivering and clenching his fists. He slung a stone out into the water, watched it splash and strode off through the sand, his mind wandering to Tony's treachery, and Sheila's shrill, knee-jerk reaction. On the windy road back to the main highway, he saw an old graveyard, overrun with weeds and tall grass. He did not remember it from the first trip. Another chill passed through him, followed by a thankfulness that he was alive.

The past seemed terminally over and resolved to Greg, but he sensed no peace about the future. He visualized returning to tennis competition entirely on his own, winning a match against Sheila's new prospect, and gloating openly in front of her. There were other possibilities: school, travel, some new sort of job. The many choices, and even his freedom to make them, constituted a sort of burden. There was an element left out that he could not identify. The fuel gauge, reading EMPTY, seemed a reflection of his feelings. A bumper sticker on a Ford Compact read:

DON'T FOLLOW ME, I'M LOST

He stopped and filled the tank, remembering the promise to

his brother. The noise and bustle of the city swallowed him up, obliterating thought, dulling the senses. As he drove, his sense of unrest returned, his old haunts exerting a tremendous pull.

HAPPY HOUR! WET T-SHIRT CONTEST EVERY WEDNESDAY

The phrase *happy hour* seemed particularly ironic, as he thought about it. Scott's car idled at a light beside another hot spot.

KAMIKAZE NIGHT SPECIAL! ALL DRINKS $1
FEMALE MUD WRESTLING. FAST AND FURIOUS!

He recognized a girl going in, deliberated for a moment while the light was red, then changed his mind and drove on.

Scott and Laura were home. They asked about the day's events—if he had found what he was looking for. *They were,* he thought, *too interested, too concerned.* He began to feel defensive again.

He told them, "To tell you the truth, I don't know what I'm going to do."

23

E lton had entertained a secret fear that in spite of all prayer and preparations, the people of Seattle would stay away from the Crusade in droves. In Birmingham, Boise, or Tulsa, they would flock to such an event, but not, he imagined, in the Pacific Northwest. Therefore, the numbers in attendance surprised him: the open stadium filled almost to capacity with people of all ages and descriptions. Elton read the faces of those who passed by: some eager and enthusiastic; some skeptical and aloof; others whose faces expressed sadness and grief; and a few enigmatic, defying analysis. Some had obviously been brought along; others were curious spectators who had wandered in alone. He looked at his wife, seated beside him. She seemed unusually quiet. Reverend Wharton waved to them from below, as he escorted a group from the church to their seats. It was he who invoked God's blessing on the gathering.

The songs and hymns seemed a bit odd at first, as though the stadium were not the proper place for the activity.

They all stood and sang as one:

> He is Lord, He is Lord
> He is risen from the dead
> And He is Lord
> Every knee shall bow,
> Every tongue confess
> That Jesus Christ is Lord.

A choir performed some special numbers; testimonies were given. Bev Shea, a regular member of the Crusade team, sang a slow, gentle piece that Elton found quite touching.

"Oh, he's so *good!*" Anne exclaimed.

The crowd burst into applause. The singer said a short word, then Graham took his place on the platform. The evangelist opened his Bible, adjusted his glasses, and began to speak.

> "I want to say tonight that in my stay in your beautiful city and in my travels in your beautiful state, I am reminded as I am in few other places that this earth on which we live is the handiwork of our God. Just yesterday, I was looking at Mount Rainier and thought to myself about the Being that would create such majesty. 'The heavens declare the glory of God,' the psalmist says. 'The firmament showeth his handiwork.'
>
> "But living inside each one of us is our spirit, our soul. This is the part of you that is made in the image and likeness of God. That is the part of you which the world cannot speak to. This is why the Bible says that the most brilliant men in all the world cannot come to God by their own knowledge or their own wisdom, however exalted it might be. By wisdom, man cannot know God. God is beyond our human understanding."

Elton took his wife's hand. The evangelist was not saying anything he had not expected, but he felt more like a member of the audience; like, even, those who wandered in out of curiosity, rather than one who had labored to make the meeting possible. As the evangelist continued, Elton pondered every word, his attention surprisingly acute.

> "But God has revealed Himself to us in nature, as I mentioned earlier, also within our conscience, and in this Book, the Bible, and, more perfectly, in the person of the Lord Jesus Christ.
> "I was walking along one day with my son, and we stepped on an anthill. Many ants died, and a lot of them were wounded. And I said, 'Wouldn't it be wonderful if we could go down there and crawl around among them and tell them that we didn't really mean to do this? We could help them rebuild their houses and bury their dead.' He thought it would be a good idea but said, 'We're too big, and they are too little.' And I said, 'That's exactly what happened. God looked upon this planet—this little speck of dust—and saw these little creatures called men and women walking around lost, away from Him. How could He communicate with them? The mighty God of heaven?' And I turned to my son and said, 'Wouldn't it be wonderful as well if we could become an ant for just a few minutes and help them?' He said, 'I think it would.' That's exactly what God did. God became a man and that's who Jesus Christ was —The God-Man."

The illustration seemed so very simple to Elton, almost better suited to a class of children than a mass gathering of mostly mature adults. He had known all this for years, but the truth of it took on a fresh, almost startling, dimension, like a poem, long forgotten, that suddenly leaps into the memory, full of life and meaning.

> "He came to take our sins on the cross, to take our judgment, to take our hell on the cross. That's why all over the world you see a cross on every Christian church, because the cross is the heart of what this Bible teaches.

And in that moment, when Christ said, 'My God, my God, why hast Thou forsaken me?' that supreme moment that none of us can penetrate, that moment that no theologian in the world has ever completely understood ... in that moment God took all the sins of the whole world and laid them upon Christ. He literally went to hell in your place."

The phrase, *the sins of the whole world*, evoked a strong imagery in Elton. He thought of the barbarities of antiquity, the empires trampling roughshod over the innocent, like runaway herds; the infanticide; the cruelties of the Middle Ages; the murders of Stalin and Hitler; the crimes committed in the name of religion or of science; the lies and deceit—the sin of an entire world over the centuries—his own sins among them. His understanding stretched to take it all in.

"No wonder the Bible says that God so *loved* the world. Think of such love! They put nails through His hands and a crown of thorns on His brow and a spike through His feet and He hung there. They laughed at Him and said, 'He saved others, why can't He save Himself?' They wondered why He didn't come down from the cross, but if He had come down from that cross, you and I would have never made it to heaven. He stayed on the cross, so you and I could be in heaven, and have eternal life, and have our sins forgiven.

"Yes, there is a mystery about it. It is a supernatural work of God in our hearts. When we repent of our sins and receive Christ as our Savior, this is what the Bible calls 'being born again.' You can't inherit this. You can be born in a Christian home but that does *not* make you a Christian. You can go to church or even be active in the church, but that is not enough. You can be baptized, but that is not enough. It was Jesus who said *you must be born again*. And these words were spoken to a religious man."

Elton had, in recent years, developed a resistance to this term *born again. It was mentioned,* he thought, *far too much on newscasts and talk shows, and had become a buzz word—a label.* It was as though the popular media had taken credit for coining the phrase that had come from Christ Himself, stripping it of all meaning.

"Many times this is like natural birth. There is a moment of conception; there are nine months of gestation, and there is actual birth. Tonight may be for you a moment of conception. It may be another step in gestation; or, it may be the actual birth. If there is one thing that I would like you to remember from this night on, it is this— that whatever you've done, whatever you've thought, whatever your condition, whoever you are, whatever feelings or struggles you may have in your heart right now—God loves you. Some of you who feel the most turned off, the most distant, are the very ones that God loves the most here tonight. And because He is God, an omnipotent God and not limited, He can concentrate on your needs and your problems as though you were the only person in the *whole world.*"

Although distant, it seemed to Elton as if the evangelist spoke directly to him, and as if the crowds melted away, leaving him there alone in the empty stadium. The course of the message adjusted to the changes in his thinking. He shifted his posture. Graham strayed from the pulpit.

"You are not just part of a crowd. You are an individual. You are here by yourself before Jesus Christ. You are alone before Him. This is something your parents can't enter into with you, nor anybody else. You must do it alone. When you go to die, you die alone. When you come to Christ, you come alone. It is a decision *you* have to make. You may be in the choir; you may be a leader in your church, but deep in your heart you are not sure of your relationship with Christ. I want you to make sure tonight. I want you to come forward. Coming forward is an outward sign to God and man that you are making an in-

186

ward commitment. I'm going to ask that we have no
music at this moment. Let's just come in the quietness
and the silence. I believe God is here with us tonight."

In the far corners of the crowd, people began to stand.
Elton struggled with a desire to join them. He thought that
his wife knew what was happening and wondered if she experienced similar feelings.

"I want to give myself to Him," Elton said, turning toward
Anne, "just as I want to give myself to you."

Her eyes brimmed with tears, and they embraced. People were standing all around them now. The last vestiges of
Elton's resistance ebbed away. He wanted to stand. He prepared to stand. The choir began to sing softly.

"Elton," Anne said, tugging on an arm, "is that Greg
down there?"

"Greg?"

He thought it strange that the name should startle him
so.

"Where? Where is Greg?"

"There," she said, pointing. "Elton, why don't you go with
him?"

Elton released Anne's hand, stood, lifted up his eyes, and
saw his son afar off.

24

Greg had been outside the stadium on a grass-covered embankment. He had resisted a hundred excuses to not attend. Phantom voices from the valleys of his mind urged him to stop, go back, go elsewhere, anywhere but *there*. No one, not even Scott and Laura, had told him to come; he had done so alone. With a great act of volition, he went as far as the doors, but remained outside. He had heard all the words of the evangelist over the loudspeakers as clearly as if he had been with the others. He had sat and listened, the babble of noises in his mind subsiding.

"Jesus said, Behold I stand at the door of your heart and knock. If anyone hears my voice and opens the door, I will come in to him."

Try as he might, Greg could not recall the last time he had heard this. The sermons and lessons of his youth seemed to have temporarily blanked out, as though he had never really listened to them at all, but flirted with some triviality instead.

> "The handle of that door is on the *inside*. You must turn it, yourself. This is not something you can completely fathom with your mind. You must come with your *heart* and your mind. You don't have to have it all settled intellectually—*but you do have to want Him in your life*! It doesn't matter if you are a Catholic, an agnostic, a Protestant, a Mormon, or a Jew—whatever your background. I'm not asking you to join any church. I'm asking you to allow *Jesus Christ* into your life."

Greg got up and entered the stadium. He stood in the highest row, above the others. The crowd was quiet. People were standing, going forward. He saw the evangelist on the distant platform raise his hands as he spoke.

> "We've all lived so many lives. We've all done many things we regret. We may be confused and uncertain about our lives. He will bring us assurance. The glory of Christ is that He offers complete freedom from guilt tonight. He offers total forgiveness of everything in the past."

Greg savored the words. They seemed more than collections of letters and sounds describing vague concepts.

More people were standing, going forward. A crowd formed at the front, near the platform. None of the explanations of sociologists and psychologists for the act seemed to have any validity just then. It all seemed so plain to Greg. People—old and young, smart and stupid, sophisticated and otherwise—all heard and received a simple message that met a deep need. And they responded to this message as countless others had throughout the ages. Greg counted himself among them and started forward by himself, alone.

He made his way down the steps, unaware that anyone saw him, thinking only of the commitment he wanted to make. Oblivius of his injured shoulder, he made his way through the crowd, and finally jumped over the railing, onto the stadium floor.

As Greg reached the floor, he made out a tall, familiar figure, wearing a navy-blue suit. They saw each other and stopped, standing some yards apart.

Elton remained still. Greg approached slowly, aware of the sound of his own footsteps, squinting into the strong stadium lights. His father's face bore an expression which at once combined relief, happiness, even joy.

"Will you stand by me?"

Greg had spoken the words without thinking, voice trembling slightly, as though they had been lines from a script, the only lines he knew. Elton clasped an arm around him.

"I'll be right beside you, son."

From another area of the arena, Scott had left Laura and the Robinsons and started running toward his father and brother. Breathless, he caught up to them. For a brief instant, they embraced, then arm in arm, the Stuart men strode forward.

They took their place with the others. The evangelist led them in prayer, then read verses from the Scriptures. A tidal wave of emotion broke loose among some of the people. Greg felt a deep serenity. He looked at Elton. He had never seen his father cry before.

Behind them, in the next wave pressing forward, were Anne Stuart, smiling through her tears, and the equally moved Laura Jaffe and Doreen Robinson—all ready to make their own commitments.

He started early the next moring, just after Scott had left for school. It was an unusually clear day. Shafts of light beamed into the apartment. He made breakfast, then put everything away, washing the dishes, some of them having been stacked dirty for several days.

Surprising, he told himself, *how few possessions he had left in the world.* He packed them all up into a bundle:

some clothes, a couple of books, a radio, his tennis racket. He looked around the ragged, little flat for the last time—at the books, the posters, the walls peeling like sunburn. He scribbled a note and left it on the table:

GOING HOME

His belongings were a bit unwieldy, but he decided to walk the three miles to Capitol Hill. Since the previous evening, he felt as if he were completing some long journey, and like a marathoner he wanted to finish it—on his own steam. As he moved through the city some people studied him with inquiring looks as though he might be a vagrant, but their stares didn't bother him. His eyes were on other things—the blueness of the sky, the crimson of some roses hugging a trellis, the freshness of the morning air. Never had the earth or the people that inhabited it looked so alive or so beautiful. At a cascading fountain, he stopped to rest. There, a smiling old woman tenderly fed pigeons. A child with a sun-bright yellow balloon ran ahead of his indulgent mother.

After splashing his face with water from the pool, he got back on his feet and continued his march. There was a spring in his step and he completely forgot his still-tender arm. As he moved closer to home, familiar landmarks popped into view and old childhood memories flooded his mind.

He took his time, examining the familiar dwellings, striding slowly up to his own.

Greg stood a moment at the front gate, then made his way slowly up the walk to the brick steps as his mind sorted through the flood of memories. There was something about the front door that evoked some long-forgotten incident—a skit, a play of some kind in which he had participated, most likely as a child—the details of which had escaped him. He thought he saw his mother through a window, as he walked between the white columns and into the house. The prodigal had made his curtain call at last. He passed through the heavy oak door and closed it behind him.